something like hope

something like hope

SHAWN GOODMAN

DELACORTE PRESS

All rights reserved. Published in the United States by Delacorte Press, an imprint of Random House Children's Books, a division of Random House, Inc., New York.

Delacorte Press is a registered trademark and the colophon is a trademark of Random House, Inc.

Visit us on the Web! www.randomhouse.com/teens
Educators and librarians, for a variety of teaching tools, visit us at www.randomhouse.com/teachers

Library of Congress Cataloging-in-Publication Data
Goodman, Shawn.
Something like hope / by Shawn Goodman. — 1st ed.
p.   cm.
Summary: Shavonne, a fierce, desperate seventeen-year-old in juvenile lockup, wants to turn her life around before her eighteenth birthday, but corrupt guards, out-of-control girls, and shadows from her past make her task seem impossible.
ISBN: 978-0-385-73939-9 (hc)
ISBN: 978-0-385-90786-6 (lib. bdg.)
ISBN: 978-0-375-89752-8 (ebook)
[1. Juvenile delinquents—Fiction. 2. Juvenile detention homes—Fiction.
3. Emotional problems—Fiction. 4. Family problems—Fiction.
5. African Americans—Fiction.]   I. Title.
PZ7.G61442So 2011   [Fic]—dc22   2009053657

The text of this book is set in 12.25-point Adobe Caslon.
Book design by Vikki Sheatsley

Printed in the United States of America
10 9 8 7 6 5 4
First Edition

This book is for the 93,000 girls and boys who occupied residential centers at the time of writing. May your stories be heard.

acknowledgments

Thanks to my wife, Jennifer Goodman, for her endless support and encouragement, and also for reading as though the safety of the universe depended on it. Thanks to Alexi Zentner, friend and most excellent advisor; Oliver French; B. G. Downing; Dana Robson; Ella Blue and Poppy Jane; Seth Fishman, my agent; Stephanie Lane Elliott, my editor; and Krista Vitola, editorial assistant.

something like hope

1

Lying on the cold hard floor of a locked room, I wish. Is it bad to wish? It feels bad, but only because my wishes drift away. They escape from me and go wherever wishes go. Where do wishes go? Better places, I hope.

Right now I am wishing to get out of here, to go far away where nobody knows me. Maybe a big city where I could blend in and walk for miles through streets crowded with anonymous people. I could listen to the cars and buses, and smell the food from the hot dog carts and pizza stands. I could get a job in an office in a nice building and work hard. With my paychecks I would buy expensive clothes: skirts, blouses, and sweater sets, all with matching shoes. And I would find an apartment, a studio where I'm the only one with a key and I can decorate it and keep it clean. I will have a down comforter on the bed and lots of soft pillows and a tortoiseshell cat that will sleep with me and I will be warm and safe and happy.

I keep trying to add more wishes, but they don't take hold. I concentrate hard, to keep the fantasy together: matching dishes, a soft rug by the bed, real furniture. But it all fades. Thick cotton bath towels and a dish of little soaps shaped like fish and shells, and still it goes away. Wishes. Dreams. People. They go away from me. And nothing remains except this cold hard floor and me.

2

How long have I been in this room? It seems like a long time, but I can't remember. I run my tongue over the jagged edge of my tooth and feel white-hot pain—and then I remember . . . stealing Ms. Williams's sandwich . . . busting her pretty face with my elbow in a fight. I got in some good blows until they took me down. I know I should feel something, like regret or remorse. But too much has happened, and I am empty inside, like a boarded-up house with no furniture, no pictures of smiling, happy people on the walls. Maybe the fight was a way to feel something, to know that I am still here and that I still matter. But I am afraid that maybe I don't matter, because I can't seem to get out of this place.

I get up from the floor and sit on a yellow plywood bench next to a stainless steel toilet/drinking fountain combo. It smells faintly of disinfectant, and I wonder if I will have to stay here long enough to use it. I wrap my arms around myself even though I am not cold. I try to focus my mind on something good, but it's hard. After a while, I find a good memory.

It's a warm summer evening, the kind of weather you get before a thunderstorm, when the air is so still and you can almost feel electricity in it. And there's the sweet heavy smell of ozone. All these businesspeople are hurrying to get home before the rain because they have expensive dry-clean-only suits that shouldn't get wet. And their hair, with all the styling gel and mousse in it, will get messed up, too. But my mom isn't hurrying. She's holding my hand and we're walking slowly, like we don't care where we're going or when we'll get there.

I think I am happy, because there's no knot in my stomach, no fear of what will come next. I feel warm and good and safe. I skip along to keep up with my mother's long easy strides. She swings my arm and sings, "I can see clearly now the rain is gone."

Her voice is beautiful and clear. She sings out loud to me and to everyone around us, like we're stars on a movie set. But really she's singing *for* me, because she loves me. Even if it's just for the moment, even if it's just because she's high on crack and feeling good, my mother loves me. She sings, "It's gonna be a bright, bright, sunshiny day." And I love her back. I squeeze her hand in return because, for this single moment in time, I love her too.

3

The new shrink, a fat white guy, comes in to see me. He's wearing baggy mismatched clothes, and glasses with thick tinted lenses that make it hard to see his eyes. He enters the room and walks toward the bench in tiny steps, keeping his arms in close with his pinky fingers sticking out. It's like he's holding those little delicate teacups, one stuck on each pinky. In a strange way he's graceful, like a hippo or a manatee in the water. Maybe he was a very small man all his life and then woke up one day in a big body.

"Hello, Shavonne. I'm Mr. Delpopolo. I'm here to talk to you about what happened earlier today."

I am still sitting on that plywood bench, eating what's left over from Ms. Williams's sandwich (hidden in my pocket throughout the whole fight). When he tells me his name I laugh out loud, spitting a piece of turkey onto the black and white checkered linoleum floor. I'm not even sure what's so funny. Maybe it's the strangeness of this guy with his goofy clothes and ridiculous name. Maybe it's because I've been locked in a room for hours and am going a little crazy. He smiles and says, "I know. Some name, eh?"

I give him my meanest, coldest stare, the one that made the old shrink look away at his art posters on the wall. What does he think he'll do—just walk in here and make friends? Well, *screw him*. I've seen too many people like this guy before, and not a single one has helped me. They talk nice and get you to open up, to soften, and then they leave. They forget about you. They go home to their own children or they take new jobs. Better jobs, working with kids who aren't criminals.

"Fuck you," I say. "Fuck you and your stupid name. I don't have anything to say."

He just smiles and ignores my words. He points at the bit of turkey on the floor.

"Is that from the famous sandwich I've heard about?"

"Maybe it is," I snarl.

He doesn't seem bothered by my attitude.

"You must have been very hungry. Or perhaps you were concerned about Ms. Williams's cholesterol, what with the bacon and mayonnaise in the sandwich. Is that why you stole it?" He arches one of his bushy eyebrows above the rim of his glasses. I wonder if he's making a joke, but he shows no emotion. No smile, no chuckle, and of course I can't see his eyes through those dark lenses. A big fat mystery stuffed into a bad suit. But it *is* funny, and I find myself laughing again, though I catch myself quickly.

"Did you say your name's *Mr.* Delpopolo? You don't have a PhD?" I say this because shrinks keep track of each other and their degrees. Plus it's good to change the subject. That way you become the asker of the questions. And the asker of the questions has control.

"We can discuss my credentials some other time. Maybe in a couple of days when I'm able to talk with you again. I wanted to introduce myself and I guess I've already done that so I'll leave. Enjoy that sandwich. You certainly paid for it."

As he walks away, I throw the rest of the sandwich at his fat ass; incredibly, I miss. He doesn't notice, or else pretends not to. That pisses me off even more, because I really wanted to eat it, and now it's ruined.

4

Almost a week has passed, so I guess Mr. Delpopolo lied about talking to me in a couple of days. I think he waited so long on purpose, just to make me mad. It's not like I *was* waiting or anything. Well, I kind of was, but only out of boredom.

The guard brings me downstairs to the admin wing. I enter Delpopolo's office and eye him coolly; he launches right into the usual shrink bullshit. Rules and confidentiality and therapeutic goals. But his heart isn't in it. He looks tired and worn out; his clothes are even sloppier and more wrinkled than the last time I saw him.

I look around at the walls, which are painted industrial green and pocked with chips and nail holes. They are bare except for two black-and-white photos. They look like they've been torn from a magazine: one of Gandhi, one of Einstein. Missing are the family pictures, knickknacks, and other crap shrinks usually keep around. But there is one thing: a ceramic coffee mug that says *World's Greatest Dad.* It's white with red lettering. The kind you can buy in any junk store for three dollars.

I bring my attention back to his little intro, which I've heard before and which I think is a load of shit. In the Center, guards and shrinks and teachers all put your business out there. They gossip about kids, each other, even the director, Mr. Slater. Especially Mr. Slater. And this guy wants me to be reassured because of his rules and "confidentiality"?

"How can you possibly help me?" I ask. "You're a mess. Why are you even working in this place—did you get fired from a *real* job?"

He smiles. "You want me to answer those questions?"

I shrug.

"Okay, here goes. I don't know if I can help you. Yes, I am a mess. I work here because, strangely, I get along okay with kids. And maybe."

"Maybe?"

"Maybe I was fired from a real job." He says it like he's not even embarrassed.

"What job?" I ask, interested now in spite of myself.

"I was a teacher. At a college."

"Oh," I say. I don't think he looks like a college professor, though I've never seen one. College professors should be older, wiser-looking. Better dressed. "So why did they fire you?"

He shifts in his seat and says, "Never mind. Now it's my turn to ask questions. How come you can't finish your program here?"

"Who says I can't finish it? I can get out of this place anytime I want to."

"So then why don't you want to get out of here?"

"I didn't say that." I am no longer interested in talking to this guy. He's twisting my words around and it pisses me off. "What if I don't want to talk to you anymore? What if I don't want help?"

"Let's just skip this part, okay?" His words suggest a hint of frustration, but he still looks calm.

"Who says I need help? You think I'm crazy or mentally ill or something? What'd they tell you? PTSD? Depression? A little intermittent explosive disorder? Borderline personality disorder? Which one do you think it is, *Mr.* Delpopolo?" I know that I should shut up, that I'm out of line, but I can't stop. I don't know why I talk like this. It doesn't make sense to, except that it's just how I am. "You people think you know so goddamn much. You don't know shit."

Then the strangest thing happens. Mr. Delpopolo slumps in his chair and sighs. I swear he looks sad. Not angry. Not frustrated. Not busy and out of time, but sad. He takes off his glasses and looks right at me, and I notice the heavy dark bags under his eyes. They are very plain eyes, brown and deep-set. And I see in them now that he too is troubled.

Maybe he's sad because he knows I need help but am

beyond helping. How can he know that? And if he does, then how can he get up and walk right past me out of the office without really trying? He doesn't even look at me or say goodbye. Instead, he calls one of the goons over and says, "We're done for today. When she's calm, please tell her that I'll see her in another two weeks."

Why doesn't he tell *me* this? He knows I'm right here and I can hear him, but he doesn't even look at me before he leaves.

5

I'm so sad. I feel like crying, but nothing comes out. My roommate, Cinda, tries to comfort me. Cinda, the freckled pixie who hears voices and pulls her hair out in frizzy clumps. Cinda, who takes five different kinds of meds and sometimes cuts herself. Cinda, who asks me hundreds of questions.

"Shavonne, why are you sad? Is it because of your daughter? Do you miss her? I would too, because I saw her picture and she's *soooo* cute. Do you want to talk about it? I saved some of my meds if you want to take them."

I tell her to mind her own business. The last thing I need is some crazy girl's pity. Like she can do anything for me anyway. She's maybe the one person in this place who's worse off than me.

Cinda says really strange things that don't make any sense, like she really loves everybody, or she's going to burn the place down on Easter. She doesn't mean it. But once you say things like that, you can't unsay them, and then there are consequences. For Cinda the consequences are that she has to stay locked up for a long, long time.

But Cinda is actually my friend. She's amazing at doing hair, and braids mine almost every night. She sits me on the floor in front of her bed and lets her fingers go like magic through my hair, twisting and crossing, twisting and crossing. Sometimes I lean back and pretend that I'm at home—even though I don't have a home—and that it's my mother who's braiding my hair. And even though it's just Cinda, it feels kind of nice to have someone fussing over me.

Cinda says nice things too. Like that my hair is strong and beautiful and I should be proud of it. "I wish I had hair like yours," she says. "You know those other girls are so jealous because they have to use weaves and strengtheners to get that look."

The guards say Cinda's been here longer than anybody else—three years. It's mainly because she has nowhere to go. They say the psychiatric hospitals won't take her because she's violent, and the group homes and residential centers won't take her because she's crazy and belongs in a psychiatric hospital. Also, she's set several places on fire, which doesn't make her very marketable.

But I want to get back to the crying. I think it has something to do with my session with Mr. Delpopolo. I think he's trying to use his psychological bullshit to break me down. I certainly don't intend to let this happen, but then again, I'm tired of holding secrets in. I'm sick of them. They make me sick. It's like drinking poison and not being able to throw it up, waiting quietly for the tell-tale signs that death is coming, the dark lines inching up your veins.

I won't go on about this, because I don't like self-pity in other people, and I hate it in myself. But I don't know if I can deal with all this. I've been numb for so long and this asshole, Delpopolo, is messing it all up. He has no fucking clue. You go opening doors that are supposed to stay closed and you end up like Cinda. Does he want to do that to me? Have me go crazy and take a million meds that make me sleep and drool? He couldn't survive a day in my shoes. Fuck him.

6

This whole mess started with a lie. Not a big one, but still a lie. I don't want to think of myself as a liar, but maybe I am.

"No, Ms. Williams, I didn't take your sandwich. I been busy at my desk working, see?"

I put on my most innocent face, which I must admit isn't very innocent. Then I sat back to watch the show. All the other girls watched too. They're all bored and mean-spirited, just as eager to see a fight as I am. Ms. Williams closed her eyes ever so briefly in silent irritation. She knew what I was doing but couldn't help playing along . . . her role in my game. And that's exactly the point, it was *my* game.

Ms. Williams's long fake eyelashes gently touched her cheeks, and in that instant, she looked pretty and perfect and soft. I wanted to freeze the moment and think of her like that always, her beautiful dark complexion, her woven hair coiled neatly on top of her small round head. Her hands rested firmly on her full hips, and I thought she looked like a mother who was angry—a good mother, who gets angry but would never hit you or say nasty things. She just wants you to know she's angry and then everything will go back to normal.

I let myself go further into the daydream and imagined Ms. Williams as *my* mother. She was angry with me but ready to forgive. She said, "It's okay, Shavonne. I know everything that happened and it's okay. I still love you. You're my baby! I'll always love you. No matter what." In the dream she smiled and placed one small hand on my cheek. It felt warm and good, like stepping into the sun when you're cold. It was so real I forgot where I was.

I forgot all about the Center and the other girls. I wanted to fall down on my knees and say to Ms. Williams, "Please . . ." Please what? Will you be my mother? Will you love me? No. I wasn't playing that. Hell no.

I stopped this thinking because it's pathetic. Ms. Williams isn't my mother and never will be. My mother is on drugs. She is a prostitute. And in that one heartbeat, the fantasy went away and I fell hard, like I was a piece of soft fruit hitting the tile floor. I snapped out of it in time to realize that I was in trouble. Because Ms. Williams is no one to be trifled with, which is exactly why I was messing with her. Everyone knew damn well that I took her sandwich. And I knew that my small and stupid lie would send her over the edge. In here it's always the small stupid stuff that sends a person over the edge.

16

This was when I failed to notice the signs of attack from Ms. Williams. I didn't see her pretty head move from side to side, as if to say, "Oh no, girl . . . you just crossed that line and now look out 'cause here it comes." I didn't even hear the first words out of her shapely lipsticked mouth. All I caught was the end part, when she found her rhythm and the words became bullets, tearing me apart like a paper target.

". . . lyin', cheatin', selfish, ungrateful, ignorant, grimy, sandwich-stealin', disrespectful . . . 'Stead of doing what you gotta do to get yourself outta here, you blame every-body else . . . and never think nothin' 'bout your own child and who's gonna be her momma when they lock you up for good in prison!"

That was the signal. It was my turn, and I was going to act out *my* part. As the rage rose up—because what she said was the truth (especially the last part)—I flipped over my desk and screamed, "Shut up! Shut up!" The desk hit the floor with a terrific crash. That's when the giant, Kowalski, grabbed me from behind. His hot meaty hand gripped my shoulder, and I jerked my arm away violently. I wasn't even thinking, just reacting, and my elbow con-nected with something solid. I hoped it was Kowalski's face. But then a woman shrieked in pain and I realized, too late, that I had hurt Ms. Williams. Someone big and strong hooked my arms behind me and threw me down, face-first. Both of my front teeth broke and blood filled my mouth. It tasted metallic and then salty. The pain was instant and searing. And I realized that *that* was what I

17

had been waiting for—a kind of release. That was what I needed. Pain. Punishment. Resolution. Call it whatever you want.

I screamed and thrashed until the other guards arrived and cuffed my hands behind my back. Somebody put their knee into my spine because I was trying to buck them off. Then I was still. Peace overtook me, though I knew it would be short-lived. All the shit that was building up faded away. The bad voices faded away. The bad memories faded away. The Center faded away. I closed my eyes and dreamed of nothing, the kind of dream you have before you're born and after you die.

7

I'm at my formal hearing for the sandwich incident. Ms. Williams's face is bruised. She's got on a lot of makeup to cover the marks, but I can still tell because she doesn't look as pretty. Her face is lopsided, with one eye and one cheek swollen. I get this sick feeling in my stomach when I see her because I don't want to think of myself as someone who would do that. But I did. The proof is right in front of me.

Ms. Williams has nothing to do with my problems. She's not responsible for me being locked up or how I feel. If she's guilty of anything, it's being nice. She was with me when I gave birth to my daughter at the county hospital. She held my hand and let me squeeze hers as hard as I could and said in a soft, sweet voice, "It's okay, baby. You can do this. I know you can, Shavonne, because you're strong and because you already love this baby." She really said those things to me and this is how I pay her back—with a messed-up face.

I want to stand up and say, "Yes, I did it. I am bad and violent and psycho. I deserve whatever punishment you give me. I'll take it even though I know it won't make up for what I've done." Because I don't know why I do what I do. It doesn't make sense, and this scares me. But then I think of my daughter, Jasmine, and how I'll never get to see her again if I plead guilty straight up. So I do what I'm best at: I lie.

I say to the whole committee, "I did it. I stole Ms. Williams's sandwich. But I only did it because I was so hungry because I was pregnant. Or at least, I was pretty sure I was pregnant."

I tell them that I had sex with one of the guards (not true) and missed two periods (partly true, because I missed one due to stress). I say that the guard told me to keep my mouth shut because he could get fired or go to jail (this is a total lie).

I say that I stole the sandwich on impulse because I was hungry and it smelled good. (The guards aren't supposed to eat on the units in front of us. Mention of this casts doubt on Ms. Williams, just like in those court movies where the evil lawyer wins the case by discrediting the witness.) I wasn't able to sleep, and then I passed some blood but it was different from my period, I add.

Then come the questions. Some of the people here know I'm full of shit, but they have to ask anyway. The

20

director, Mr. Slater, says, "Didn't you tell anybody? What about your roommate?"

I answer quickly to get it over with, wondering how long I can go on with this story—and how long it will take for it to catch up with me (because it always does). "No, I didn't tell anybody."

"Nobody? Not even your counselor?" Slater again. He's furious that there's a problem he can't make go away.

"No. Nobody."

"Why not?"

"Because I was scared. I kept hoping that, somehow, it would go away."

"How do you know you are pregnant? As far as I know, none of the nurses did any blood work."

"I know, believe me. I've had a child before, Mr. Slater. I know what it feels like. Do you want me to give you the details?"

"No, that won't be necessary. But it is necessary for you to tell us who the father of this alleged baby is."

"I'm not telling you his name."

Everybody in the room sighs. They don't want to go through all this. They want to finish their shifts and go home.

Mr. Slater gets a nasty edge to his voice. "Why? Because you want to protect him? Let me tell you something, young lady. You're in no position to protect anybody else. You should be worrying about yourself."

"He told me he'd deny it. Besides, I don't want to get him fired. He said he loves me."

Slater rubs his temples. It's too illogical for him, this feminine drama. His face is red, and I can tell he wants to scream at me. He might even want to slap me around. It must take tremendous control not to.

The nurse takes over the questioning and asks me about an exam. "We're going to have to get you in to see a gynecologist, Shavonne. Today."

"No!" I shout. "Nobody's looking inside of me. Give me papers to sign if you want, but I'm not letting anybody check me out. If you don't believe me, fine. Give me any kind of punishment you want, but I'm not going through any GYN exam. Hell no."

It's an awful lie but I think it will work, which is all that matters right now. To prove me wrong (and charge me with Assault), the Center will have to do an investigation. That, in turn, will look bad for Mr. Slater, no matter what the outcome. It's bad PR. So I give them a way out and tell them that I just want to get back to normal and that as far as I'm concerned, nothing really happened. I make it easy for them by saying, "How about I take back the whole thing? Can you drop it then? I'll say it was just a lie, and you can punish me for lying and that will be the end of it."

Mr. Slater's eyes get wide and he flashes a big fake smile, like he's so happy that we've reached an understanding. He says, "Of course you should recant if it's not true. Is that what you're saying?"

As I play along with the sick game I worked so hard to set up, it occurs to me that I am getting further and further away from my release. *Why do I keep messing up so badly?* At the end of the day, sitting in my room with Cinda braiding my hair yet again, I face the truth: I have spent my last three birthdays locked up in different placements. I have a child who doesn't know me. And there are so many other bad things I can't even write about. Actually, I think I am falling apart.

8

I enter Delpopolo's office and sit across from him. He doesn't look as tired this time. He greets me politely.

"Hello, Shavonne."

"Hello, Mr. Delpopolo."

"It's been almost two weeks."

"Yes, I guess it has."

It goes on like this for several ridiculous minutes. Then he stops the chitchat. He folds his arms on his chest and leans back in the office chair. I hear the spring groaning under his weight. I imagine the tension in the spring increasing until it explodes. It will snap under the pressure and shoot into the wall at about a hundred miles per hour. But the spring holds. And the real tension is in me, because I can't stand the silence, the waiting.

"What? What do you want?" I say.

"I don't want anything." He is calm and still. He looks genuinely confused by the tone of my question. Or is he pretending? It's hard to tell.

"You had me brought down here and you're not even going to talk to me?"

"What are you expecting me to say?"

"Hell, I don't know. Aren't you supposed to ask questions or give me some lecture about what's wrong with me?"

"No. I'm not supposed to do anything other than meet with you every week, so long as you're willing."

He's playing games with me. He's trying to get me to talk first and tell him why I'm messed up. But I'm not telling him. I'm not telling anyone. I say, "Come on, Mr. Delpopolo. Ask your questions and let's get this over with. You want to know about the hearing. If it's true or not, right?"

I am expecting him to lie, to say he's not involved and Mr. Slater never asked him to talk to me. But he doesn't lie.

"Okay. Fair enough. I doubt there's any point in keeping things from you. I *was* asked to talk with you about the hearing, but we don't have to. It's your business."

"What do you mean it's my business?"

"It's your business. It doesn't concern me."

"If one of these guards raped me and got me pregnant and I lost the baby from being hit and thrown on the floor, that doesn't concern you? Are you out of your fucking mind?"

"If you tell me that story, then it concerns me. But you *haven't* told it to me. Until you do, I'll let the others handle it."

The exchange goes on like this for some time. He's careful with his words, like he's trying not to disrespect me, and I start to think that he might be okay. That maybe he's got no agenda, he isn't lying. Or maybe I'm so desperate to have someone to talk to that I'm falling for his stupid shrink tricks.

I want to believe that he can understand. That I can tell him more. I want to tell him about me. I want to tell him the truly awful things and have him say, "It's okay, Shavonne. It's not your fault. You're going to be just fine." Maybe he can hear what I have to say and handle it. But then again, how could he? Why am I thinking like this? I'm all mixed up and I want to cry. But instead I flip out. "Get the fuck out of here," this voice inside of me says. "Get out now. You're in danger. Something bad is going to happen if you don't leave."

I hear this voice sometimes when there's a lot of stress. I think it wants to help me, but I'm not sure. I don't always listen to it. But this time I do. It tells me to scream, so I scream and scream and scream. It sounds like I'm angry, but I'm really scared. I don't know what is happening to me, and I don't know what to do anymore.

9

There's a new guard here named Cyrus Jacobs. He's a real hillbilly. He wears a long scraggly goatee and talks with a southern twang.

Cyrus says he's from the South, but he won't say exactly where. The Center has this rule about employees "disclosing personal information" to residents. The idea is if a guard tells about his family or something, one of us could use it against him. They also say it blurs the "boundaries," which is not professional. The Center is very big on "boundaries." Not many of the guards follow these rules, but I guess Cyrus does.

I wouldn't pay any attention to Cyrus if it weren't for his interest in the pair of geese out on the pond. Every day when we walk across the grounds for meals, he makes us stop to look at the birds.

"They're Canada geese," he told us once. The birds are enormous and loud. Nothing like the pigeons and plain old ducks I used to see before I arrived at the Center. Cyrus just stares at the geese and forgets about his job. This is dangerous, since he's supposed to be watching us to make sure we don't break the line and run away.

Just as some of the girls start getting edgy (no doubt thinking about running), Cyrus calls us over and says, "Hey, girls, you see them geese?"

Tyreena, big, black, and bold as hell, puts one hand on her hip and says, "Yeah, so what? What's the big deal about a couple of gooses? Man, it's cold out here and you gonna stop and ax us about some dang birds?"

The way Tyreena tells it, she is locked up for infidelity. That means she caught her boyfriend cheating and taught him a lesson by cutting the girl's face up with a utility knife. If you ask her about it, she'll say, "My box cutter taught her stank ass not to be pokin' her titties where they don't belong." Nice. But believe it or not, in her world, Tyreena was playing by the rules. Seeing another girl edge in on your action is more than enough reason to go after her with a knife. I'm not saying I'd handle the problem that way, but plenty of girls would.

Cyrus breaks his gaze from the pond and returns to earth. His voice stiffens. "Fall in line, then, girls. Walk!" He's all business for the next few minutes, and he looks like his feelings are hurt. Then, just before we go inside to lunch, he stops the line and says, "Tyreena, those geese are mating pairs. They mate for life. They're here to nest and raise their young. I want to tell y'all this because some of y'all might be here long enough to see their babies get born, if the foxes and coyotes don't get 'em first. It might be fun to watch and it could make the time go faster."

As we enter the cafeteria, most of the girls roll their eyes or suck their teeth in disgust at the idea of some backward hillbilly cracker fuck trying to engage us hardened city kids in some nature goose freak show. Tyreena, never one to let another have the last word, says, "What you mean they mating pairs and they mate for life? What you mean, *Cyrus*?" Tyreena exaggerates every sound in his name to make fun of it, challenge him, and question his credibility. Tyreena is no one to mess with. She's not very bright, but she can be tough as hell both with words and with fists.

It interests me to watch Cyrus handle himself in this small drama. The whole cafeteria is quiet with suspense. This bumpkin has been challenged, and no one, not even the other guards, is going to help him out. *Sink or swim, Cyrus.*

Finally he says, "It means they're faithful to one another for the rest of their lives. It means that if one dies, the other will be alone until *it* dies." The silence continues. I can tell what everyone is thinking. *For life? Really? That's incredible. Unimaginable!* Because no one is faithful. Not parents, teachers, guards, boyfriends, or girlfriends. No one. What's it feel like to know that someone in your life is that faithful? Is that what real love is?

I want to pull Cyrus aside and ask him these questions.

Maybe he knows. Maybe this stupid-looking guy learned all this from hunting and fishing and watching geese. Maybe he knows something that no one else does.

But the other girls don't seem to be thinking these things. They just look at Tyreena as if to ask, "Well, ain't you got nothing more to say? You gonna let the cracker have the last word?"

When she talks, Tyreena is indignant. "You mean to tell me that man goose gonna stay by hisself if his woman goose dies? I don't believe that. You believe that, Kiki?"

Kiki does not. Kiki and Tyreena are girlfriends, meaning they are gay (at least when they're in lockup). Kiki is good-natured, gullible, and likable. She's very pretty, too. In the Center, she's considered a good catch.

Cyrus closes the argument by adding, "It's true. I didn't make that up. Check with your life science teacher if you don't believe me." Cyrus seems to miss the real point of the argument. It has little to do with the truth of what he said.

Kiki, always one to help out, says, "Well, *I* ain't never met no man like that. Cyrus, maybe you should be teaching this nature shit, I mean stuff, to some boys. So they know how to treat us right!"

This draws laughter from everybody and ends the drama, but not before my impression of the geese changes completely. To be honest, I'd never really noticed them before. Sure, they're in the pond every day, paddling around with their big webbed feet. But who gives a shit about some stupid birds, right?

30

Then I think about my parents, and Tyreena's and Kiki's, too. Our moms just knew our dads casually and they decided to fuck each other, have babies, then go their separate ways. Or maybe our dads cheated, drank, smoked crack, beat our moms up, went to jail, got out, and died of liver disease or from getting shot. That's probably closer to the truth. More than half of the girls at the Center don't even know their fathers. At most they have a name, a worn-out old picture, or an address of a prison somewhere.

Faithful for life. I can't decide if it's beautiful or ridiculous. In any event, the cafeteria fills with voices, conversations, and the sounds of all of us making it through the day, guards and kids alike. For every conflict that ends peacefully, there are ten violent ones. Every day two or three girls hit the floor for some reason or other. Maybe it's for blurting something out, cursing, or refusing to sit down. But it can also be for nothing. Maybe a guard is having a shitty day or just got a drunk driving ticket. She might take it out on you until you slip and mutter something under your breath. Or maybe you just roll your eyes and she sees it and says, "Shut up! You talkin' back? Stand against that wall!" Then you're fucked. Inevitably, she'll hook your arms behind your back and hip-toss you onto your face. Eyes get blackened, chins split open, and cheeks burned from rubbing on the floor. "One more word out of you, Shavonne, and you'll hit that floor. Is that what you want?"

No, Ms. Choi. I don't want to hit the floor.

10

I overhear Ms. Choi talking to another guard. "You know that big fat man, Delpopolo? The psychologist?"

"Yeah. So?"

"Well, I heard his wife left him for this guy she met on the Internet. Came home one day with papers from a lawyer and said she's leaving. Took their little girl with her too."

"Damn. That's cold. Where'd you hear that?"

"Corrine in personnel. But don't tell nobody."

It made me mad to hear these women gossiping about Mr. D like he was a sucker or something. Maybe his wife was a real bitch and there was nothing he could do about it, but all I could think of was that pathetic coffee mug on his desk. *World's Greatest Dad.* The only thing left of his life with his family. You know what the worst part is? I'll bet he *is* the world's greatest dad. I'll bet he used to play with his daughter and have tea parties and read her fairy tales and call her princess. I'll bet he used to take her out to restaurants, just the two of them, and let her order anything on the menu, even waffles and ice cream or onion rings and a chocolate milk shake. I can see the two of them sitting on the same side of the booth at Denny's, leaning up against each other playing tic-tac-toe on napkins with those little crayons they give you. He probably let her win and then looked proud at how clever she was.

I wonder if I'll ever get to do those things with my daughter. It seems so far away. Like it's impossible, or like it's something that only other people could do. Someone like me, but not me—a girl who's older, prettier, and certainly a better person. No secrets inside of her. Nothing dark and dangerous that can break through the surface and destroy everything.

11

Today I watch the geese out my bedroom window. I tell Cinda everything I've learned about them from Cyrus. She's fascinated and sits cross-legged on her bed, rocking excitedly. She asks lots of questions, only a few of which I'm able to answer. Which is the female? How long will she nest? How many eggs? How will she eat? I point to the male, which circles slowly in the pond. We watch for over half an hour and see him catch two little fish, which he brings over to his mate.

It's exciting and yet painful at the same time. These two Canada geese outside our window have what we all want. They're free to take off at any time *and* they have each other. I don't think Cinda processes it on this level, though. She keeps saying they're beautiful, and that they need to be looked over and protected. "Nothing's gonna happen to them, Shavonne—you won't let anything happen to them, will you?"

I'm telling you, she's close to the edge. In an instant, she becomes totally obsessed. It's my mistake for showing her, but who knew she'd get so crazy over the damn things? I had to tell her because I'm just so bored and lonely and miserable. It's normal for girls our age to talk about what happens during the day, right?

We stay up late, talking about how much we'd like to fly away to a new place. Cinda says she wants to go to Key West and live in a pink bungalow and get a job styling hair. She says there are lots of gay men in Key West and that's good because they're fun and she feels safe around them. Her bungalow will be decorated with mermaids and unicorns and faux fur. Pink and purple everywhere. Glow-in-the-dark constellation stickers for the bedroom ceiling so she can lie awake at night with her friends and stargaze.

Cinda says she'll always have friends around because she can't stand to be alone. She will have guest rooms and pull-out couches and an old-fashioned record player with lots of vinyl from the eighties and nineties. It really sounds like fun, and I tell her I'll come visit her, even though that's more of a fantasy than the pink bungalow in Key West. Of all the kids in the Center, I know that Cinda and I are the least likely to leave and make it on our own.

Then it's my turn. And because it's just Cinda and it's two o'clock in the morning, I tell her my fly-away fantasy, the one I started in room confinement. In it, I'm twenty-five years old and I live in a big city where nobody knows me except the people I work with. I've got business suits and really nice shoes. And even though I'm just a secretary,

I'm good at my job. People treat me nicely and sometimes ask me for help.

My apartment is small but beautiful. It is clean. It is orderly. There's matching furniture, thick soft carpets, and a big television I can watch from a giant canopy bed with a real down comforter on it. The kitchen is filled with nice things too: matching dishes, shiny pots and pans with real copper bottoms, even spices. I have the spices organized alphabetically in cute little bottles. I can cook whatever I want whenever I want. And the best part is that, at the end of each week, I go to the mall and use some of my paycheck for dinner and a movie as a reward for being normal. That's it. That's all I really want.

Cinda says it's a good fantasy, and I realize it's the first time in weeks somebody has said something nice to me. I think I will sleep well tonight.

12

Delpopolo tells me we don't have to talk so much if it upsets me. Instead, he'll give me writing assignments. The first one is to write about a single good childhood memory. I tell him that I don't have any good memories, but he ignores my comment.

"It needs to be at least one page long, and when I read it, it should seem real and honest. So include as much detail as you can." He also says he doesn't want to keep the assignments. "They're really for you, but you can read them to me in place of us screaming at each other, okay?" He smiles just to let me know that he's kidding and not being disrespectful. I appreciate the gesture, however small. After a while in the Center you suspect everyone is trying to fuck with you and cut you down.

The memory: I am a little girl, swimming off a wooden dock with my father. It's a reunion of my family on my father's side, but I hardly know anyone. I don't think my father got along with his family, but at this party, everyone seems happy. We are having a picnic next to a lake, and there is so much food: fried chicken, potato salad, greens, hot dogs and hamburgers. There's a couple of pies, too, and I can't wait to eat them.

My father is big and strong, and his body is covered with tattoos and scars. He has just been released from prison, but no one talks to me about this. They do, however, tell me that I resemble my mother, and this makes everyone look sideways at each other, the way people do when there's stuff going on that you're too young to understand.

After eating, I go down to the edge of the lake and dip my feet in. The water is cold enough to leave goose bumps, but it is very hot outside and it feels good. I am too skinny to fill out my bathing suit, and my father says, "Girl, you need to eat more." I am not used to him, and the attention is almost too much, too good. And being around these kind people, even if I don't really know them, is so nice. They keep asking me if I want more soda or pie. They call me lovely and beautiful.

The absolute best part is when my father decides to come swimming with me. He gives me his good leather basketball to use as a float because I can't swim. "Be careful," he says.

I jump in, but the ball pops up without me. And just as I start to go under and swallow the water, my dad's arm plunges into the dark green water and he pulls me up. He swims me over to the basketball, makes sure I'm okay, and asks if I want to keep swimming. I nod.

The next time, he holds my hand and says, "Ready, set, go!" We jump together, knees drawn up in the air, mad grins on our faces, water flying off our nappy heads in silvery beads. The drops of water hang in the air. They catch the sun's rays and bend them into different colors, and it's just me and my dad playing together. The sky is extra blue with cottony clouds, and he loves me. I am his little girl.

Another memory: my dad no longer lives with us. He moved out of state and doesn't call or send money anymore. I'm alone with my baby brother. My mother is out, but I don't know where because she doesn't tell me. My brother clings to me for warmth and comfort. It's cold and he doesn't have a sweater or even toys. No stuffed bears or soft blankets. I carry him everywhere and he cries when I put him down—so I don't put him down.

I make up a game and pretend that I'm his mother. Kind of like what other little girls do with their favorite dolls.

"Do you want me to be your mommy? Okay, I'll be your mommy. Are you a good baby? Marcus, have you been a good baby today? I think you have."

Marcus puts his head down on me and falls asleep. He is warm and soft and he loves me. Even though I am only a little girl myself, I can tell that he loves me and trusts me, and this fills my six-year-old soul with happiness. I lie back on the filthy sofa and pull an old blanket over us. I am cold and tired and my belly growls for food, but for the moment I am content, because there is someone in the world who loves me. Someone who needs me.

Marcus's little hand wraps around my pointer finger, and I feel the tremendous power of this bond. His tiny fingers wrapped around my own. A hand inside another hand. I watch his eyelids flutter with dreams. I kiss his forehead and say, "I love you, little baby. Momma loves you."

13

Ms. Choi is pissed today. She will take out her seething hatred on one of us. We all wonder who it will be. Coffee? China? Kiki? Tyreena? Me? No. It will be Samantha, this skinny Hispanic girl with wild frizzed-out hair and a bad case of ADHD.

"Samantha, put your hand down and turn in. I ain't answerin' no more of your dang questions."

"But Ms. Choi, I gotta go to the bathroom. Goddamn, you gotta let me go. The ombudsman said."

Samantha is hyperactive and special ed, always bouncing off the walls and getting on people's nerves. She's harmless, though. One of those kids who talks tough when she's threatened but never does anything.

"We just had a bathroom break. How come you got to go whenever there's schoolwork?"

"But Ms. Choi, I really gotta go. It's for real! I ain't messin' around, I really gotta pee."

"You know, Samantha, maybe if you spent more time studyin' you wouldn't act so retarded. Now face forward and do your work. We'll have another bathroom break in a while."

The special ed teacher, Ms. Sheffield, pretends not to hear the retard comment. Ms. Sheffield is even more frightened of Ms. Choi than she is of us kids. Instead of reminding Ms. Choi that Samantha is a bed wetter and sometimes has accidents in the daytime, she shuffles her papers together and leaves.

Samantha tries to keep her cool. For about eight seconds.

"Maybe I am retarded, but at least I ain't no fat bitch!" She mutters it under her breath, but everyone hears. Tyreena, Kiki, and the others all say, "Oooh! No she didn't!" as though they're on the set of the Jerry Springer show. It's all very predictable.

Ms. Choi has a way of knowing just how to push people's buttons. With Samantha it's the retard thing. With another girl it's calling her baldheaded or the daughter of a whore. ("You know the apple don't fall far from the tree, especially when Shaquana and her momma be out there sellin' they asses together.") Nothing is off limits with Ms. Choi.

In the end, she beats Samantha's ass for her comments. The 250-pound woman hooks the girl's arms behind her back and hip-tosses her on her face. Once Samantha's down, Ms. Choi levers her skinny arms as high as they'll go without breaking and continues to torment her.

"See, girl? That's what you get for runnin' your mouth.

Always talkin'. You wanna talk now? You still got somethin' to say?"

During the takedown part, Samantha crashes to the floor on her face with the big woman on top of her. Her chin cracks hard and blood drips onto the dirty white tiles.

"I can't fucking breathe! You're hurting me! Owww! Shit! Owww!"

"Oh yeah? If you can't breathe then how come you're able to scream so damn loud? If it's one thing I can't stand it's a liar. Liars be runnin' they mouths all day and they can't even back it up 'cause it's all bullcrap." When Ms. Choi gets fired up, her language gets more street.

This only brings out more fight in Samantha, which I think is the point. She thrashes and kicks and screams under Ms. Choi's weight. Her blood smears everywhere as she wails in a god-awful way. A couple of minutes later, four guards respond. One grabs Samantha's legs so she can't kick. Another cuffs her hands behind her back; the two other guards stand next to the pileup with their arms crossed, looking tough and official.

Samantha continues to fight like crazy until the cuffs are on. She almost bucks Ms. Choi off her. She has that wiry strength that only crazy people have. The rest of us are sitting at our desks, trying to stay calm. It's disturbing when a girl gets taken down like that. It feels wrong to just sit there and do nothing, but if you try and help, *you* get slammed. Then they give you a rule violation for inciting a riot. That adds thirty days to your sentence and means you have to go before the review board, like when

I stole the sandwich and hit Ms. Williams. Go to the review board too many times, and they can send you to adult corrections.

As Samantha screams, so do I—inside my head. I yell, "Stop it! Stop it!" over and over. I don't even know if I'm yelling for the guards to stop hurting Samantha or if I'm yelling for Samantha to stop fighting and screaming. It doesn't matter. I just can't take being around any more of it. My fists are balled tight, my ragged fingernails digging into my palms. In my mind I try to block out what's happening.

I put my head down and hum real loud to drown out the noise. Michelle, who sits next to me, begins to rock in her chair. She rubs a pencil eraser back and forth across her wrist to burn her skin. Michelle has cuts and burns all over her arms, legs, neck, and chest. The behavior specialist woman made a plan to get her to quit, but it obviously hasn't worked.

Finally, Samantha stops struggling and cries, "I can't take this no more. I can't. Somebody call my mommy because I can't be here no more. This place is no good for me! You people ain't even helping me. You're hurting me. I'm not getting better, I'm getting worse. I need help. Please. Somebody help me!"

It makes me sick, the idea of all these full-grown men and women beating the shit out of this girl. Samantha talks shit and annoys people. But that's hardly a reason to torment her and bust up her chin.

Later, we line up and move to the cafeteria for dinner. They're serving burritos with Spanish rice and nachos. Even though it's our favorite meal, no one eats. Samantha is getting stitched up in the clinic, which is close enough to hear her whining and crying. It goes on forever: "I want to go home!" and "I want my mommy!"

Kiki and Tyreena mumble, "Shoot. Shut the fuck up, Samantha. We heard your stupid ass already." But I notice they don't touch their food either.

Only Ms. Choi eats. She pretends not to notice the screaming. She smiles and sings to herself, "Don't worry. Be happy!" She asks me to get a plate for Samantha in case she's hungry. Then she proceeds to eat Samantha's dinner. Kiki rolls her eyes in a visible display of disgust, as if to say, "Dang! That's mad grimy, eatin' that girl's food." Ms. Choi notices the look and says, "Kiki, you got somethin' to say, then say it. Otherwise shut your face, girl. I already had enough drama for one day. Don't nobody need no more."

The rest of us try to bury our noses in our books, but Ms. Choi won't let us. Instead, she bullies us into phony conversations about Beyoncé and Mary J. Blige. She turns on her charm and tells jokes and funny stories, making a false display of everyone being cool with each other. It feels even more wrong than the actual beating.

Samantha comes back to the unit after dinner. She has a gauze pad taped over her chin. She's spaced out on painkillers. It's strange to see her sit there quietly. Her hands don't fidget, her skinny butt doesn't slide all over the chair, and you can almost read the thoughts in her head: "I want to go home. I want my mommy."

And even though it's selfish to think of myself, the thought forms: "At least she has a mommy. At least she'll go home to someone when this is all over. She'll get off the van with her garbage bag full of state-issue crap clothes, and her mother and grandma and aunt will hug her and cry with happiness. They'll all board the city bus and go back to their shit hole apartment in the projects and have a big party with fifty brothers, sisters, aunts and uncles, cousins, and friends. Old women will bring casserole dishes of plantains, rice and beans, stewed chicken, and flan for dessert. And, in their own imperfect and beautiful way, these people will love Samantha because they don't care if she's imperfect herself. They don't even know what a learning disability is, or conduct disorder, or ADHD. All they know is that Samantha is one of them and they love her."

14

Susan, my daughter's DSS worker, calls me on the phone today. Department of Social Services is the agency that takes kids away when they're abused or neglected. They save them from abuse by putting them in foster homes where they're abused and neglected worse, this time by strangers.

I'm not kidding. Many of us girls in here have been abused in foster care. For the foster fathers and foster brothers and foster uncles, it's like they've just won the lottery and got their very own thirteen-year-old sex toy. It happens two or three times and then you see the writing on the walls: "Oh, this is how it's gonna be." You run away. Then you get picked up for hooking or boosting stuff, because if you're fourteen and homeless, there are only two ways to get by: sell your ass or sell drugs.

I am still in DSS custody, and so is my daughter. Maybe my mom was in social services, too, but I'm not sure. She never talked about her childhood except to say that it sucked.

I gave birth to Jasmine while I was locked up. Because I still had time to serve, Jasmine got placed in a foster home. I have to say it's a good home, and the single black woman, Connie, loves Jasmine and treats her well. I'm glad for this, but it kills me too, because I know in my mind and in my heart that this woman is a better mother than I could ever be.

I handle this poison truth by being mean to the DSS worker. I treat Susan like she's responsible for my daughter being where she is. I know it's stupid and wrong, but I can't help it. And I'm just frigid enough with Connie. But I can't show too much attitude, because she'll tell Susan. Then Susan will, in turn, tell the family court judge that I'm uncooperative. That's how you lose your rights as a parent. Imagine, losing your parental rights! Sometimes, though, I wish a judge could've terminated *my* parents' rights. Maybe if it had been done when I was little and cute, I could have been adopted by a real family.

Anyway, Connie calls every week to tell me how Jasmine is doing. "Jasmine sang her first song yesterday." "Jasmine ate a whole hot dog by herself." "Jasmine learned how to ride a tricycle." After this torture I get to say hi to my baby. She says, "Hi, Mommy!" in the sweetest voice, but I know that Connie is behind her whispering what to say. She probably has a picture of me handy to prep Jasmine before the calls. She might say, "Look, sweetie, this is your mommy! Remember your mommy?"

These phone calls take place on Thursdays. That's the day that I don't eat. I don't do it to lose weight or punish myself. My reason is far more practical. I fast because the calls make me so nervous that I throw up whatever's in my stomach. Then, later, I usually get into a fight or a take-down. It's just better not to eat.

So this social worker, Susan, is only a few years older than I am. She just graduated from college and has that fresh, bright-eyed look that makes me want to scream. She tries to "relate" to me. Not that that's such a ridiculous thing to try . . . it's just that we're sooo different and she pretends it doesn't matter. I remind her constantly that it does. Either she doesn't get it (what did they teach her in that college, anyway?) or she pretends that she doesn't care. Hell, she shops at the Gap and drives a lime-green VW Bug! Everything about her is so damn cheerful and cute, even the way she talks about how Jasmine and I can be to-gether when I get out.

Time to grow the fuck up, Susan. There is no getting out for kids like me. I will *not* get to be with my daughter. That possibility disappeared long ago. Two years ago, to be exact, on June 8. When I gave birth to Jasmine in the county hospital, I was almost sixteen, and I got to nurse her and hold her and soothe her to sleep for two days. I sang her songs and kissed her a thousand times on the head and cheeks. I changed her diaper even when it was dry. I tried to memorize her smell, that beautiful warm new-baby smell. I tried to memorize all the details: the softness of her skin, the downy hair on the nape of her neck, the shape of her nose and her chin. The gorgeous nut-brown color of her skin. I wanted to take her to every room in the hospital and hold her up to each patient and say, "This is my daughter. I am her mother and she is my daughter. Promise me that you'll remember this. Promise!" I wanted to make them say it—to hear the words and make it real.

And when it was time, the nurses wrapped my baby up and let me say goodbye. My breasts were swollen and ached for their one real purpose. Unknowingly, I cupped them with my hands and let loose the most God-awful scream you have ever heard. Ms. Williams had started to put the cuffs and shackles on me, but she wasn't able to finish. She started crying too, and then pulled me toward her. We both fell to the floor and cried like that for a long time. I don't know what she was crying for. Maybe it was for all the black and brown babies who grow up without parents. Maybe she just felt sorry for me. I don't know. Eventually, an orderly pried me off Ms. Williams and laid me down on a gurney and wheeled me to the psych ward. I stayed there for five weeks.

15

It's Samantha's sixteenth birthday today. She's excited because it means she gets to go home soon. She keeps telling everyone they can have a piece of her cake.

Tyreena says, "Damn, girl, you mad stupid. Don't you know that everybody get a piece a cake on a birthday?"

Kiki, the kinder of the two, snaps at Tyreena. "Why you gotta be so mean? She happy it's her birthday and you be beastin' on her. Say you sorry."

"Shit. I ain't sayin' I'm sorry when I'm not really sorry, 'cause that's mad two-faced. Kiki, you *know* I don't lie."

"That's different from a lie, and you know it. Say you sorry, Tyreena!" Kiki puts her hands on her hips to show she's mad.

"How you gonna stick up for her? Ain't no one stick up for me when I was a little girl and there wasn't no cake! And my mom's boyfriend come out callin' me bitches and hoes!"

Kiki throws her hands up in the air and walks away. "Um, excuse me. Did anybody say they wanted to therapize you right now, Tyreena? This ain't about you, so be quiet."

"You want me to be quiet, or apologize? How can I apologize if I'm quiet? That don't make sense."

The argument goes on. But in the end, nobody gets to eat Samantha's birthday cake. After dinner, Ms. Choi announces to all of us, "You ain't gettin' no cake after that bullcrap you pulled the other day. We don't reward negative behavior. It don't matter what day it is. If you actin' the fool, there ain't gonna be no cake."

Ms. Choi boosts up the volume of her voice to drown out the sighs and grumbling. A chubby girl with her hair in puffs says something about how it's in the resident handbook that every girl gets a cake on her birthday.

"Now, girls, we all know what the rules says about birthday cakes. They say Samantha has to get a cake for her birthday, but it don't say *when* she has to get it. So what we're gonna do is put it in the fridge for now. And tomorrow, if Samantha chooses to act her age and stop with the negativity, *then* we'll eat the cake."

Samantha goes absolutely berserk. She knows that Ms. Choi and the others will eat her cake after their shift is over. It doesn't matter how good she is. It's not about her behavior anymore, or the cake. It's about humiliation. And Samantha knows all about this.

"Motherfucker! I'll kill you, you fucking pig. *¡Puta!*"

In a blind panic, Samantha charges across the cafeteria at Ms. Choi. She makes it about three steps before the giant, Kowalski, grabs her and, in a smooth powerful wrestling-type move, throws her down. Samantha struggles but only manages to reopen her stitches. It's a bloody mess, and we get sent to bed early while Samantha goes to the hospital to get stitched up by a real doctor.

These are the worst kinds of punishments, because they're senseless. Getting slammed for calling someone a fat bitch at least makes a certain amount of sense. But losing your birthday cake because the night staff are going to eat it because you got slammed for calling someone a fat bitch . . . that makes no sense.

And on top of that, there's nothing any of us can do for Samantha. Her will is being broken, and it makes me sad to watch it happen. And how quickly sad becomes angry.

16

Mr. Delpopolo sits down at my table at lunch today. This is weird because nobody ever eats lunch with us except the guards.

"Hello, girls," he says, as though it's completely natural and normal for him to be here. His ass is so big it hardly fits on the small round stool that's bolted to the table. The girls laugh.

Mr. D. senses the joke and says, "Yeah, I know. I'll have to have this thing surgically removed at the end of the meal." Everyone laughs, but this time they do it along with Mr. D. It's a neat trick he pulled, and I'll have to remember it.

"What's that?" Tyreena demands as she practically pokes her nose into his food. Delpopolo doesn't seem to mind the rudeness.

"It's gumbo."

"What? I ain't never heard of gumbo. What's in it?"

"Do you really want to know? I'll tell you, but you might find it boring."

"I axed, didn't I? If I didn't want to know I wouldn't have axed."

Delpopolo talks all about the ingredients: okra, sausage, shrimp, tomatoes, etc. Then he tells us about the secret ingredient, filé powder, which comes from ground sassafras. "If it's made with browned flour instead of filé," he says, "then it's not *real* gumbo."

"Can I try some?" Cinda asks. Delpopolo promises to bring enough in for everyone the following week. Then he asks, "What do all of you like to eat?"

We go around the table. Kiki says, "My moms makes macaroni and cheese—the real kind where it's baked and the edges are all crispy and browned." We all ooh and aah because baked macaroni is the best. Tyreena says she cooks soul food with her grandma: fried chicken and black-eyed peas and greens and sweet potato pie for dessert. Cinda tells us about the time her school band went to Red Lobster and she ate cheese biscuits and lobster soup.

Tyreena is outraged. "You go to Red Lobster and order soup and biscuits? Girl, you is whack!" Cinda makes a face at Tyreena and tells her *she's* whack. We all talk and laugh and bicker. It is really kind of nice and fun. Like a normal conversation.

17

Court hearing today. It's called an EOP, short for Extension of Placement. The Center can extend your stay for intervals of six or twelve months until you turn eighteen. Some girls stay after eighteen if they've done really serious crimes, like manslaughter, weapons offenses, fire setting, sex abuse.

The hearing is routine and will go quickly. Probably last about five minutes once we get in there. My law guardian is a total asshole. He looks like he slept in his clothes and he may be drunk. He has foul breath, and I have to turn my head when he talks to me.

"Sign the waiver, it's best for you," he says.

"No thank you, mister."

"Look, the judge is going to extend your placement anyway. Why not save us all some time?"

"I'm in no hurry, sir."

He starts to get frustrated and mutters under his

breath. Something like "For Christ's sake, you fucking kids are all alike."

Most girls sign the waiver, but it's really a stupid move. You gain nothing by it. And if you refuse to sign, there's always the chance that, during a hearing, the judge will get pissed at the Center and cut you loose. It happens sometimes because the Center doesn't present well in court. Case managers show up without their paperwork and can't remember even the most basic facts about us girls.

But it doesn't work out that way for me. The judge remembers me and orders twelve more months, and gives me a lecture about taking responsibility. Then it's back to the Center for a strip search. After any trips or visits you have to go in this empty room and take off your clothes. Then they make you stand with your hands against the wall. I won't go into the details, but they check in all the places.

No matter how many times you go through it, it's still humiliating. If you have any self-esteem or dignity, you lose it. You don't want to talk to anyone, even people you like. And from that point on, you see the guard who searched you as a pervert, even though it's always a woman and she usually dislikes it as much as you do.

18

Ms. Choi is back at work today after her pass days. Samantha is real quiet even though Ms. Choi ignores her. But after breakfast, Ms. Choi says casually to the other guard, Ms. Haley, that she's going to meet with Samantha to "process" the incident in the cafeteria. She says it loud enough for all of us to hear. I think, *Oh, shit. Here it comes again. Why can't she just leave this poor girl alone?*

Choi says, "Now, Ms. Haley, you *know* I'm gonna have me a talk with girlfriend about that bullcrap the other day." She gives a dirty look over her shoulder at Samantha and smiles like it's a game and she's having fun. Ms. Haley nods in agreement.

"Oh, me and Samantha gonna have us a good sit-down talk, 'cause Ms. Choi don't tolerate no bullcrap like that. There ain't gonna be no more of that."

Choi turns her chair to get our attention. "You see,

girls, you got to give respect in order to get it back. And don't none of y'all know nothin' about respect, otherwise y'all wouldn't be in this place. What you gotta do is learn the basics that your parents didn't never teach you, like please and thank you and no ma'am. . . ."

It goes on like this until Samantha starts to crack. She's scared about having this "talk" with Ms. Choi. I know just how she feels. When you get taken down real bad, the last thing you want to do is face the guard who did it. You want to avoid them for a couple of weeks, not even look at them if you don't have to.

Samantha starts rocking in her chair. She makes a moaning noise and puts her head in her hands. I cringe from the awful sound and want to scream or hit someone. I don't understand why this happens to me. Why do I go off my fucking rocker every time some other girl does? I might even want to hit Samantha. Or one of the guards. I'm not sure.

Choi walks over to Samantha and says in her gentle voice, "Come on now, Samantha, honey. Come on and let's talk. It'll be okay." Samantha gets up and follows Ms. Choi into the staff office. I listen for signs of trouble, but all I hear is Ms. Choi. She's using her teaching voice now, the one that is loud but compassionate, righteous but not at all condemning. This is the voice she uses to draw you back to her after breaking you down. She only uses it when you're exhausted and can't fight anymore. You give in because you're so damn tired, and you can't take any more pain.

I know Samantha will give in. It isn't her fault. She's just a skinny kid who's scared and can't read or write or remember her times tables. She can't see through Choi and her simple mind-fuck. All she sees is the sudden kindness, a blessing totally unrelated to the earlier abuse.

And that's good for Samantha, because it means she's just dumb enough to stop fighting and get out of here. She'll start following the rules. She'll leave the Center, go home to her grandma, quit school, get pregnant, and sign up for Social Security disability benefits. Happily ever after, right? I wish I could do the same. I wish I could go back to a loving grandma and live happily ever after.

19

"I want you to write a list of all the things you feel guilty about or ashamed of," Delpopolo tells me.

"Why?"

"For now, it's my job to worry about why. Your job is to write honestly."

"Can I call you Mr. D? Because Delpopolo is too damn long." Changing the subject. The assignment scares me and I'm just stalling.

"Sure. If it's easier."

"What if it's easier for me to call you an old bastard or something?" I'm pushing it now, desperate to avoid the rest of the session. I'm hoping he'll kick me out, even though I don't really want that.

"Well, then I insist you change it to *Mr.* Old Bastard, okay? Listen, Shavonne. You've been doing a good job here. I know this is difficult."

"You have no idea."

"No. I don't, and I hope you won't hold that against me."

Strange. I *have* held that against people. But the others have always lied about it—said they understood when I knew and *they* knew that they didn't really understand. Couldn't understand. I look hard at Mr. D and wonder if the stuff Ms. Choi said about him is true. It probably is, because he looks pathetic as far as men go. He's at least seventy pounds overweight and is bald except for a few strands combed over the top of his head. But there's something undeniably kind and good about him too. Like he won't hurt you because he can't—because it's just not in him.

And maybe that's why he let his wife take his kid and all the money—because he just didn't have it in him to fight her. Tyreena always says people mistake kindness for weakness. Maybe she's right.

"Do you think people mistake kindness for weakness?" I ask.

After some thought he says, "Yes. Some do."

He takes his tinted glasses off and looks past me, no longer responding to my question. He's lost in the thousand-mile stare, focused on some vague point on the far wall. And when his eyes refocus and meet mine, I see that they are the plainest brown eyes I've ever seen. No— they are simply eyes that you don't want to look at for very long because they are sad. Unbelievably sad, like they've soaked up more sadness than they can hold and it's all threatening to spill out at any moment in a flood of hot salty tears.

I look hard at the man behind the glasses and come close to tears myself. But I don't cry for anyone, least of all paid shrinks. Even so, it is a moment of understanding that only two truly miserable people can share. And I am grateful for it, brief as it is.

20

I've been thinking about my last session with Mr. D. I am really afraid to face him again, because I know that something happened between us—some kind of understanding. It was no therapist trick, either. It was an honest moment. You know, where two people stop pretending for a second and let each other see who they really are. I haven't ever experienced that before and it's weird. Not weird in a sexual way, but just weird, like I don't know what to do now. Am I supposed to trust him? Be honest with him? And what if he pretends that nothing happened, that it's business as usual: him asking me questions and me trying to evade them? I don't think I can handle that.

But I learn that Delpopolo does not pretend.

"Shavonne, I'm sorry about what happened last session," he says.

"Why? Why are you sorry? You didn't do anything wrong."

"I'm afraid I did. I broke the rules."

"What rules?"

"My rules. About letting my feelings interfere. My problems. You shouldn't have to deal with that, and I'm sorry."

I am stunned. Silent. I honestly don't know what to say. He's sorry for showing his feelings?

"It's all right, Mr. D. Really. It's okay, and I accept your apology even though I don't think it's necessary."

"Thank you, Shavonne."

And we sit in silence for several minutes. It is a comfortable silence, without any tension or anger or pressure to speak. And in that silence, I can feel something growing between us. Friendship? Understanding? I don't know. Whatever it is . . . I think it's nice.

21

I'm working on my writing assignment, but I'm going to shred the list when I'm done. The words jump off the page and scream at me. "Hey, you!" they say. "You're garbage. You're worthless. You beat up Ms. Williams after she was nice to you. You called your mother a crack whore and hung up on her when she phoned you from rehab, trying to apologize. You . . ." And that's where it stops. I can't even write the last thing on the list. Because if I write it, then it becomes real. And I've been trying for so long to make it not be real.

I don't know if Mr. D has any experience with this stuff. I don't think he knows that there are some things that are beyond forgiveness. And there are some of us who can't be redeemed. No second chances.

I'm crying now and I can't stop. I feel so bad. I think I want to die. I *do* want to die. But I can't even think straight enough to put together a plan. Why hasn't Delpopolo talked to me yet? What the fuck is he waiting for? This is all his fault because of his stupid assignment. You're not supposed to think about this stuff. You're supposed to let the past be the past. You're only supposed to worry about what's going on at the moment. That's how you take care of yourself. That's what they tell us in our groups.

I think I need serious medication. I hate meds, but I hurt so badly that I can't stand it anymore. I'm hoping for fires and earthquakes and more terrorist attacks. I'm praying to die in my sleep and disappear into the cold fog that floats in over the pond some nights. I'll become fog and change into a million particles of water and stop being me. I don't want to be me anymore.

22

I'm sick, but not the mental kind of way (for a change). I've got the flu. I feel like shit, but I get to spend the day in the clinic. The nurses are nice. They give me ginger ale and broth.

Even though I hate my mother, I wonder about her. Is she alive? Is she safe? Does she think about me anymore? Does she even remember that she has a daughter? I want her to be here on the edge of the cot. I want her to be like she is in my old pictures, before crack: pretty and soft, her skin smooth and beautiful, not all ashy and ruined.

I want her to put a cool washcloth on my forehead and say things like "Poor dear" and "Sweetheart." I want her to bring me soup and crackers and a glass of ginger ale. I want her to worry about me and be proud of me and braid my hair just like Cinda does. I want her to take me shopping for school clothes and sit next to me on a bench in the mall, sharing a milk shake. I want her to pull me toward her on the bench so we'll lean against each other, feeling each other's weight and pressure. Is that love, feeling the weight of someone leaning against you—someone who is another person but still a part of you? I think it must be. And I wonder what that must feel like, the weight of love.

Questions. I drive myself half crazy with questions that can never be answered. Why can't my mother love me? Is that too damn much to ask? You hear that, God? I want a fucking mother. A real mother, not some toothless bald-headed crack whore disguised as my mother. But that's all I get, right? That's all I deserve. Less than I deserve, because she's not even here. It's just me, cold and forgotten in my small state bed with thin blankets. If I get pneumonia and die tonight, it won't matter. No one will care, including me.

But I don't die. And in the morning, Mr. D comes to visit and he brings me a couple of magazines, some apple juice, and a container of chicken noodle soup. The magazines are the wrong kind (*Popular Science* and some women's fitness magazine), and I wonder how he ever managed to get a job working with girls. But it's so nice of him. Nobody ever bought me something just to be nice. The juice and soup go down easy and make me feel better.

Mr. D pulls up a chair and says, "Want some company?"

"Sure," I tell him. "That would be nice."

"You get any sleep last night?" he asks.

"A bit. Mr. D, thanks for these things. I'm not used to people being so nice. I don't even know what to say."

"You said thanks. That will do. How's the soup?"

"It's good. You didn't make it, did you?"

"No. I don't know how to make soup. But my mother, her name was Damaris, she made the best soup you've ever tasted. Avgolemono. It's Greek soup, with egg and lemon. She used to make it for me whenever I was sick, and I swear it worked. Two bowls and you're all fixed up."

"She liked to cook for you?"

"She liked to cook for everybody. If someone came to rob the house, she would cook for them. 'Sit and eat,' she'd say. 'What's the hurry? Have some stuffed grape leaves and a bowl of soup. You can do your robbing later.' "

"She sounds nice."

"Yeah. She was. Only there was so much food in the house and so many cousins and aunts and uncles telling crazy stories, I never bothered to play sports or make friends. It was so much fun to stay inside and eat and listen. It's how I got to be so fat."

We talk some more and I tell Mr. D that I've been thinking about my mother—how bad it makes me feel knowing that she doesn't want me or doesn't even care about me.

"Do you think she'll ever change?" he asks.

"No. I know she won't. Not ever."

"Then what can you do about it?"

"I don't know. Nothing, I guess."

"There's always something you can do."

"What?"

"How about you rest up and we'll start on it when you're well."

23

"Shavonne, imagine there's a big red button on my desk. It's all lit up like something from a video game. If you press it, then you get snuffed out instantly, removed from existence without any pain at all. But that would be the end of your life and you couldn't get it back. Would you press it?"

For the hundredth time I think about disappearing. Not necessarily dying, but disappearing. I think about Jasmine growing up with her foster mother, who is good and kind. I think about everyone who will be happier, better off when I'm gone. But I'm still afraid to say those things aloud. I'm afraid Mr. D will send me to the psych hospital or put me back on meds. So I stall—because I'm really afraid to answer the question, which means I'd push the button. I'd do it. And then I'd never have to remember the last time I saw my mother, that crazy twisted look on her face like she didn't even know who I was, didn't feel anything at all for me; like she was looking right through me, actually, out the door and down the stairs, to the alley, where some scumbag was waiting for sex.

Delpopolo wakes me from my thoughts. He says, "Okay, let's try this another way. What keeps you from doing it? Why are you still here?"

"I don't know." It's one of those questions that should be easy to answer, but it's not for me. "My daughter. I want to see her again."

He nods. "Anyone else?"

"I had a brother." My heart pounds because I am getting close to something dangerous. Delpopolo waits like he's got all the time in the world, like it's just a matter of waiting long enough to get me to talk. Doesn't he know I *can't* talk about this? That it's nothing against him. I just can't talk about it. Ever. My stomach cramps up and I wrap my arms around myself, desperate for even that little bit of comfort.

Delpopolo is looking right at me. I say, "Something happened to him."

And it's like a key has been turned. Instantly. All kinds of locked-up memories flood in. Memories of my brother, his little hands closing around my own little fingers. The sound of his voice as he'd make those baby words that seem so important, even though they're not real words. He'd trail off at the end like it was a question, staring right into my eyes, and I'd smile and try to guess what he was thinking, what question could be on his little one-year-old mind.

They're good memories mostly. Playing with toys I made from cardboard cereal boxes and paper-towel tubes, having tickle fests, lying down for naps together. But then these memories lead to the really bad one, my secret. And, even though it was a mistake and an accident, it's something that I can't ever say sorry for . . . because it's just too terrible. Shameful. Damning.

Mr. D. gets that far-off look again and he says something strange. He says, "It's shame that drives us, Shavonne. We are creatures made of shame and guilt." But even though he says my name, he's not really talking to me. He slumps into his chair and goes silent.

24

I'm afraid to go to sleep because I keep having nightmares. I know a trick to keep calm, though: if you draw your knees into your chest and rock, it puts you into a kind of trance that is almost soothing. I don't know where I learned this. Maybe it's just something you do when you're cracking up and nothing else helps. Because I am sick, and not in the sniffling sneezing kind of way. I don't know what's happening to me.

I hear the voice of one of my old foster mothers, but I know she's not here. It says, "Come on, girl. You go in there with Uncle Leon." She's desperate. Pleading. Her face is pinched and hollowed-out at the same time, from too much drinking and drugs. And she's close to crying . . . or cursing at me. "He'll give us fifty dollars, Shavonne. I need that money for my medicine."

I am frozen with fear.

She says, "I'll buy you some damn toys. Whatever you want."

The man's face, hopeful. My legs, like cement. Not my own. I am eleven years old, trying to figure out what's happening. I know what's happening, but I don't want to believe it. Can't believe it. But it *is* actually happening. And I am acutely aware of what I am losing—what is being taken from me forever.

25

After going back and forth about it a hundred times, I bring my "guilt list" to my next session with Delpopolo. I want him to know that I did the assignment . . . that I really am trying. But there's no way he's going to get to see it. No one's seeing it. I hold it tightly between my thumbs and forefingers, ready to tear it into tiny pieces at the slightest threat.

He points at the paper. "Shavonne, is that your homework assignment?"

"Yes."

"May I see it?"

Silence. I feel raw, ready to scream out in pain at the lightest touch, like every nerve in my body is on edge. Like this autistic boy I knew when I was at one of the psych hospitals. He could only wear really soft clothes, cotton T-shirts washed in a special detergent. One of the nurses explained that anything coarse would feel like needles to him. That's how I feel, but not my skin. Right now my heart feels hypersensitive to any criticism, like a single push or the wrong word could make me cry for days.

"I don't know if I can do this, Mr. D. Some of the stuff on this list . . . Can I just go back to my unit?"

He doesn't say anything for a long time. I think about ways to get out of that office, maybe by getting loud and causing a scene. Cursing and making threats works with most adults, but not Delpopolo. Finally, he speaks.

"How about this. You take out the list and put it in front of you. I won't look at it. When we're done we'll go to the shredder together and destroy it. What do you say?"

I think it must be a trick.

"What's the point, then? Don't you need to see it?"

"No. I don't. Especially if you're so worried about it. Now take it out and put it in front of you."

I still think it's a trick, but I take it out anyway, my curiosity about what the trick might be overcoming my fear for the moment. I open the envelope slowly, carefully, like Charlie did in that movie, *Willy Wonka & the Chocolate Factory*. Only I know what's inside and it's not a golden ticket or an invitation to something special. It's the opposite: a letter saying, "You're bad. You're garbage." It's an invitation to see, item by item, exactly why there's no hope for me.

I smooth it out on Delpopolo's desk and wait. He hands me a thick black marker. I take it, my heart pounding. I'm sweating all over.

"Now go ahead and cross out all the things on your list that other people did to you."

"What? I don't understand."

"Is being raped listed on your paper?"

"Yes." I look down at my shoes involuntarily. I tell myself to pick my head up, that I have nothing to be ashamed of. But I am ashamed, and the shame burns its way through me. It's such an automatic response and I hate myself for it. And I despise Mr. D for making me feel that way. Fat fuck! Bastard! Cocksucker! But I don't say any of these things out loud.

"Well, you can start by crossing that one off."

"But . . ."

"But what?"

"Never mind. You don't understand." Shame continues to burn through me. Remembering. Hating. I want to hate Mr. D, even though he has nothing to do with what I'm feeling.

"Maybe I don't, but that's no reason to clam up. Explain it to me, Shavonne. Those men who hurt you when you were a child, how was that your fault?"

"Because . . . It's complicated."

"Yes, I imagine it would be. Go on, though."

"Look, I was bad. I didn't listen to anybody. Like the time I stole money from one of my foster mothers and then ran away. When I got caught, they sent me to another foster home. That's when the really bad stuff happened." I took a deep breath, preparing for this last part. "If I hadn't been so bad, I wouldn't have been raped. See?"

Delpopolo doesn't speak for a couple of minutes. Then

he asks a whole string of yes-or-no questions about that particular foster home.

"Did you like it at the first foster home?"

"No."

"Did anybody there beat you?"

"My foster mother burned me with cigarettes and made me sit naked in a cold tub of water when I was bad."

"Did anybody act sexually toward you while you were there?"

"My foster mother's boyfriend and one of his friends."

The questions go on like this for several minutes. It goes so quickly that it doesn't upset me so much. It's strange; maybe because it goes fast and is so matter-of-fact. It's easier to answer yes or no without having to explain. It's not like, "Tell me about when you were raped. Tell me about when your mom abandoned you."

Mr. D says, "Adults are responsible for protecting children. The adults in your life didn't protect you. I'm not being judgmental, because maybe they tried their best. But in the end, they didn't protect you. And you weren't safe. And bad things happened to you. People did bad things to you. And the systems that were set up—cops, social services, foster care, residential centers—all failed to protect you as well.

"I don't blame you for not trusting anyone. You shouldn't. You've had to do whatever you could to keep yourself safe, and that's okay. But you have to know that none of it makes you a bad person, and you're never to blame for the mistakes or crimes adults commit. Now, cross off the things on your list that are the crimes or mistakes of adults."

I start to cry because my mind is replaying so many of these "crimes" that I have blamed myself for. Some disgusting old man took my hand and put it down his pants, told me it was a good thing when I was just old enough to know that it wasn't. I thought he picked me because he could see that I was bad. A nurse at the emergency room told me I had been raped *because* I had run away and wore makeup and tight jeans. *See what happens when you run the streets? You get what you deserve, always.* And all the times I got moved from one home to another because I let someone at school see the bruises and scars. *It's because of you that you have to live with strangers who beat you and molested you. That's what you get for sharing your business with teachers and social workers.*

This is what's playing out in my mind as I cross the items off the list, one by one. So many black lines across the paper. My chest heaves with sobs. Delpopolo gives me a box of tissues and waits. Then he asks more questions.

"How can parents take care of and protect their daughters when they're using crack?" he asks.

"They can't," I answer between sobs.

"What happens to eleven- and twelve-year-old girls when their mothers are on crack and can't protect them?"

"They get raped."

In this way, he explains why what happened to me happened. He says, "Your problems—bad dreams, anger, spacing out—they don't mean that there's anything wrong with you as a person. They're just what happens when someone lives through terrible things. They're normal reactions to a really abnormal and awful childhood." He keeps explaining and asking questions until it starts to make sense. Even hearing voices can be okay, as long as I know it's just a part of me that is trying to protect me. It's not necessarily crazy, he says. I've never had this kind of conversation before. I've thought things that were all wrong, and the other therapists just made it worse. They were more interested in the ugly details of who did what than in me as a person.

I'm not saying that Delpopolo is helping me. Because I'm no less miserable than I was before I started seeing him. If anything, I'm worse, because I've been thinking of things I never let myself think about before. But I will say that some of it makes sense. In my head it's starting to make sense. But in my heart . . . it's still confusing, and it still hurts too much.

26

Cinda is now an expert on geese. She's got a library book on North American waterfowl. Our library is mostly filled with out-of-print books that people have thrown away. There's nothing fun to read, like horror stories or sexy romances, but if you want a book on the life of Ronald Reagan or North American waterfowl, you're in business.

Cinda watches the geese through our bedroom window. If you press your face against the glass (which leaves oily nose- and fingerprints), you can see the nest. It's at the edge of the pond, a hundred feet away, close enough to count the eggs. Cinda says it's called a clutch of eggs, in this case eight. She says if you're patient enough, you can see the mother get off the nest every now and then to drink water and crap. Cinda uses these moments to count the eggs, just to make sure they're all there.

She reports to me every evening about her latest discoveries.

"Shavonne, the male caught five fish today. He ate two and gave three to the female!" "Shavonne, from my math the eggs should hatch in less than two weeks!"

In a way it's cool because it gives us something new to talk about. The geese don't have anything to do with this shitty place. They live here too, but they can fly away. Once the goslings hatch and grow, Cinda tells me, that's just what they'll do: fly away.

27

A new girl was admitted to the Center today. She's fourteen years old, from the city. Her name is Mary and she's mentally retarded. She has that fetal alcohol look, with the wide-spaced eyes and flattened nose. Her mouth hangs open and she talks with a lisp, though she doesn't talk much that I can see. Mary tells us she doesn't know why she's here and didn't do anything wrong. She says, "I want my stuffed bear, Jojo, but they won't let me have him."

Lots of girls in here are slow. They cover it by fighting or talking up the gang shit. But it's pretty obvious when someone is retarded. They can't read or tell time. The judges lock these girls up just as quickly as they do ones like Tyreena and me. Usually their crimes are prostitution or running drugs for some guy. I feel sorry for them because it's not their fault. But then again, I have enough to worry about. What the hell can I do for some retarded girl anyway?

When I look at Mary, though, all my hardness goes out the window. Right off I see that she's several months along. A skinny little thing with a big belly and swollen breasts. She has a woman's body, but her face looks like a child's. She wears this dumb smile like she trusts everyone and wants to be friends. If you could see that face, open and with the dumb fucking smile, it's as if she's been sent to this world as a test for all of us. God's saying, "Treat this girl well and in her own way, she will look after you. She will be the test of goodness among you. Love her, and above all else, protect her. Because if she is harmed . . ." That's what I'm afraid of, because this girl *will* be harmed here. I can sense it.

She stands looking straight at me, smiling, with her hands on her belly. It's the most innocent smile I've ever seen. I look away and then storm off. This girl, this Mary, is bad news. You just wait and see. She's not smart enough to protect herself, and some girl, like Coffee or China, or one of the guards, is going to use her up. And I have to either watch it all play out or get involved. Like I'm going to get involved in this Mary's shit. Fuck that. Next time she flashes me that smile I'm going to knock it off her damn face.

But at bedtime, I find myself thinking about her and her baby. I say a silent prayer for her even though I stopped believing in God a long time ago. I never pray for myself because it doesn't do any good, but maybe it can work if you do it for someone else.

28

This is my next assignment: to write about a woman I've felt safe with.

It's June 7, 2002. I'm at the hospital in the maternity ward. I'm almost sixteen years old and it's my first year in lockup. They tried to send me to a group home where I could have the baby and then learn how to be a mother, but I was too messed up. I didn't follow the rules and eventually tried to run away.

After the cops picked me up (pretty hard for a pregnant runaway to stay on the down-low; maybe I should have thought of that before I ran), they took me to the Center. I stayed there until it was time to deliver. Then, when my water broke during lunch (pizza squares and Tater Tots), they took me in shackles to the local hospital. Once I was there, the shackles came off and everybody treated me differently.

Ms. Williams stayed with me the whole time. Even

though it took twenty hours and she has children of her own to look after.

I was assigned to this big fat nurse who was also a midwife. She was the only black nurse in the whole hospital, and I think she took a special interest in me. She said some really beautiful things to me that I will never forget. Her name was Mona.

When Mona met me, she took my own bony hands in her large soft ones and said, "Child, if I'm gonna help you have this baby, then we need to git a few things straight. First off, I know where you come from. You come from that prison for kids. And that means that you done something wrong or somebody done something wrong to you. And here you are, still a child yourself, yet gettin' ready to have your own child."

I wanted to interrupt, but I found that I couldn't speak. She rubbed my hands so gently, talking in this gospel-like voice, singsongy and sweet. I just listened like a little girl at story time. Those hands of hers must have been magic.

Mona said, "Child, I done wrong too and, you know what? Don't nobody care. Least of all God. And if God don't care 'bout that, then why should any smaller peoples care? Certainly don't nobody here at this hospital care what you done. You just another woman ready to bring a new person into this world. And sugar, that's *the* most beautiful thing ever! You'll see. And when you do, I'll be right here with you." She said this last part like she knew it to be true. Like she could see the end of the story and she knew it was a good story with a happy ending. Like she was amused at my distress because she knew it would all work out.

Mona was very busy with her nurse's duties. She bustled about the delivery room and talked constantly. She gossiped about famous people like Martin Lawrence and Denzel Washington. She said she wanted to have them both as lovers: the first to make her feel good with laughter, the second to make her feel good "any damn way he wants to!" She talked about the food she cooked at home and how maybe I could come over for a holiday dinner with my baby after I got out of the Center. She said the white nurses and doctors gave her grief because she got too close to the patients. At this she huffed and said, "Shoooot, girl, you cain't get any closer to a person than when you help bring they baby into the world! Got your hands up in they business, that's how close you git! It don't make no sense *not* to get to know them and let them know you."

Then Mona sat down on the edge of my bed and took my hands in hers again. She said, "Shavonne, I am a big black woman from South Carolina. Where I come from, there's plenty of girls your age who make babies. Sometimes they married. Not often, but sometimes. And sometimes they been raped. And sometimes they been screwin' with boys because they wants to." It seemed like the more she talked to me, the heavier her accent became. I don't know if it was from the medication I had been given, but it was kind of surreal. Mona's words and voice hypnotized me. I felt warm and safe and happy.

Before I went into labor, she said, "Sugar, you listen careful to Mona now. Listen careful and remember these words. Young child, you are special because of what you been through . . . and also because of what you're gonna do in your life. I see it in your face. You're gonna have lots more troubles for sure, but I see that you're gonna grow up to be a strong and righteous woman. Strong and righteous! And you got to remember that this child that's gettin' ready to meet you is part of you. To hell with all them men that call theyselves fathers. Sperm don't mean shit! Every man's got it. This one is *your* baby. God gave her to *you*. You hear me? God gave *you* this baby girl. Now try your best to take care of her. And if you cain't take care of her, then find somebody good who will."

The strangest part is that I didn't know I was having a girl ahead of time. I didn't think Mona knew either, but I guess she did. She probably had access to some records or tests. But sometimes I like to think that she just *knew* because of something deeper. Maybe something more spiritual. Like Mona is my protector. A large black woman who is strong and righteous, like she said I'd be, but also soft and gentle. I like to think that she is still out there somewhere and that I might see her again. I still have fantasies about this.

I imagine that I wait for her outside the hospital one day. She comes out after her shift, tired, heading for the subway. I come up behind her and call her name. When she turns, I say, "Hey, Mona, you remember me?" She sees me, smiles, then takes me in her arms and holds me so tight that I can't help but feel that everything will be okay. From this point on, it will be okay. At the end of the fantasy she says something like, "Girl, where you been? How many years gone by and I been waitin' all along! Now let's go home."

29

I'm brought to answer another call from Susan, the DSS worker. After some small talk she says I've got to appear in court just before my eighteenth birthday. It's time to decide what to do with Jasmine. Guardianship, they call it.

I don't have much to say to Susan. The silence makes her nervous, I can tell. She doesn't want to end the conversation on a bad note and asks stupid questions. *How's school? Is it getting cold up there?*

I tell her I have to go.

This means I've got six months. Time is running out. I've got to fix things. I don't have a plan yet, but I've decided to get real with Mr. D. Maybe he can help me. If anyone can, it will be someone like him—someone with sad eyes and a life that's not all perfect and happy. Someone who might actually be able to understand. Not just that, but he seems to know things, like how to quiet your mind when the same crazy thoughts run over and over. Or how to accept something that isn't fair. I need to learn how to do these things. I'm going to try harder. It's a promise to myself. And to Jasmine.

30

"You have a child, right?" Delpopolo asks, but it's not really a question. "Will you tell me about her?"

"Sure, if you tell me about your kids, Mr. D."

"Okay, I have a daughter. What's your daughter's name?"

"Jasmine. She's twenty-three months old. I had her when I was almost sixteen. Yours?"

"Cynthia. She doesn't live with me anymore. I'm divorced. Do you miss Jasmine?"

I am surprised that Mr. D is telling me this much about his family. When I was sick, he told me about his mother and the soup, but that's all he's said about his personal life.

"Yes. But I never even got to know her well. I've seen her during visits, and I have some pictures. Do you miss your daughter?"

"I do. I really do. She's a terrific kid. Where's Jasmine's father?"

"I don't know. He was a loser, but because he was older and had a nice car and flashy clothes, I thought . . . I don't know what I thought. That maybe he cared about me."

"But he didn't?"

"No. Not really. He didn't even come to the hospital when she was born. Then he got arrested, and I haven't seen him or heard from him since. What about Cynthia's mother?"

"Gone away. To California." Mr. D is quiet for a minute. Then he gathers himself with what looks like tremendous effort and continues. "Tell me what's special about Jasmine."

It's the first time I've been asked this kind of question. It's such a simple question, but I don't know the answer. I can say stupid things like "she's cute" or "she's so sweet," but those are clichés.

"I don't know, Mr. D. I don't know what's special about her other than she's pure and innocent and beautiful the way all babies are. But it's so hard for me to think about her as a person, separate from me and my problems. It's all a big knot of problems."

Mr. D is quiet again, so I go on. "I'm not a good mother, Mr. D. It doesn't matter how special Jasmine is because I can't really appreciate her. If I did, we'd be together."

"I can see how you'd think that, but it's circular logic. It doesn't float."

"What do you mean, 'doesn't float'?"

"It doesn't hold water. It's no good."

"Why?"

"Because. It always leads back to the starting place. You're here because you're a bad person, because only bad people get sent here. It's circular and doesn't prove anything."

"It makes sense to me."

"Listen, do you ever have fantasies or daydreams about you and your daughter together?"

"No."

"Really?"

"I'm not lying and I'm not playing any games with you, Mr. D. I just don't think about it."

"Why?" He asks this question in the mildest and most curious way. It's like he really wants to know and isn't leading me toward some point where he'll say, "You see? That's because . . ." There's no bullshit moral or lesson. He just wants to know why.

"Because . . . I won't let myself. I want to, but there's no point."

"Why won't you let yourself have fantasies about being with your daughter?" Again with the "why's."

"Because if I can't do my job as a mother and actually be with her, then I don't deserve to have the fantasies. And there's a part of me that thinks I can't really handle it. Giving Jasmine to me would be like giving an alcoholic a drink and saying, 'Hold it, but don't taste.' "

"Okay. You won't let yourself think about your daughter because you're too afraid of the feelings that come with it. You're afraid they'll destroy you." I just look at him and say nothing. He continues.

96

"To get out of here and get back your daughter, Shavonne, you have to *feel*. You have to experience all the emotions that people have, not just anger and fear."

"You think all I feel is anger and fear?" I feel both of those emotions right now. Sweat trickles down my armpits and soaks my bra. I listen for the voice in my head to tell me to leave. But I also keep that voice at bay, because this might be my last chance. *Is it my last chance?* The voice hears this and screams at me.

"Look at him, Vonne! Is *he* strong? Can he protect you? He's getting paid, for Christ's sake! He gets a fucking check to say this shit to you." The voice is mean, driving home the points like sharp blows. "It's his *job*! You get it? It's his fucking job. He don't care about you. I'm the only one who cares about you, right Vonne?"

This is why Mr. D asked permission to talk so straight. He must have known I'd react this way. It's like I found this door where the voice lives and I want to shut that door for good, and I think Mr. D is trying to help me.

He says softly, "Shavonne, are you still here with me right now? I need you to stay here with me and talk this through."

He looks at me with concern. I'm quiet, but I've still got his question in my mind. I wait to hear the voice. It is gone. Slowly, carefully, I calm down, and it's like I'm floating back into my body that is talking to Mr. D.

"Okay, so I'm angry and scared. Lots of people are angry and scared. You mean to tell me that you're never angry and scared?"

"Yeah, I get angry and scared. But I have other feelings too. And I don't try to avoid them. Listen, Shavonne, it's not okay to be angry and scared all the time. You've got to see that."

"Or else?" I know Mr. D doesn't want to hear this from me, but I think of that voice locked in a room, the doorknob starting to turn. I picture it as an old brass knob, dented in a couple of places, cold and slippery in my hand. It turns with a slow and steady force that will soon overpower me.

"There's no 'or else.' You either choose one way or the other. And the choice sets you in a certain direction."

I close my eyes and try to focus on breathing. My balled fists tingle. Mr. D waves a hand in front of my face and says gently, "Shavonne, talk to me. I'm sitting right across from you. It's just you and me in this room."

For better or worse, I tell Mr. D about the voice and the door. I am fearful of the standard talk about medication, atypical antipsychotics, and whatever diagnosis he thinks is right for me. I could take a script for Zyprexa, which makes you gain weight, or Risperdal, which makes you lactate. It even does that to boys.

"You know, you did a good thing just now. Talking to the voice and telling it that you have things under control is a big step—that's exactly what you should do."

"You don't think I'm crazy?"

"No."

"Do you hear voices?"

"No, but I talk to myself sometimes. Listen, what does that voice usually tell you to do?"

"Run away, hit somebody, curse someone out."

"How are all those things similar?"

"Look, I don't know. Why don't you just tell me? I don't mean to be rude, but I just can't think anymore." I feel exhausted. Wrung out.

"They're all ways that kids protect themselves. When you feel threatened or in danger, does the voice protect you?"

"Yeah, I guess. So what? You talk about it almost like it's a good thing. It doesn't feel like a good thing. It feels crazy."

"It's good up to a point, if it works. But that's what we're getting at here. It no longer works. Being angry and scared, trying to squash all the other emotions, it just doesn't work for you anymore. You agree?"

I look down at my chewed-up fingernails. I agree. It makes sense. It explains a lot, but still . . . what am I supposed to do? Stop being Shavonne? How? This is the only way I know how to be. I feel so confused. I tell Mr. D that I've got a new emotion: confusion. Anger, fear, and confusion. Is this progress?

Back in my room, I stay up late waiting for the voice to say bad things about me. It will call me a liar and a stupid bitch. It will say, "You're so weak, Vonne. You shouldn't have done that, Vonne. You broke the rule, Vonne. No one can know about me."

But the voice doesn't come.

31

Cinda's gone off the deep end with the geese, naming them John and Julia. John is named after John Travolta because *Grease* is Cinda's favorite movie. She sings that one song, "We go together . . . ," about twenty times a day until China threatens to punch her. She's so damn white, she messes up the shoobie-doobie part. She can't get it right even when we coach her. Julia is named after Julia Roberts because *Pretty Woman* is Cinda's other favorite movie.

The names are harmless, I know. What's crazy is that she's got stats on the death rate of goslings. Cinda tells me that only a small percentage of the hatchlings will reach adulthood. Starvation, disease, hunters, collisions with planes. These are the risk factors. And then there are the predators: coyotes, foxes, dog packs, birds like hawks, eagles, falcons, and vultures.

When I return to my room she's crazy with fear and

manic energy. Her face is pressed against the windowpane even though it's dark out. She can't see a damn thing, but she scans the pond anyway, or the area where the pond should be.

"Shavonne, we've got to do something! John and Julia are in danger! The woods behind the parking lot are filled with predators. It's not safe. I won't let anything happen to them. Do you hear me, Shavonne?"

I hear her, all right. I hear her telling me she's going insane. She stays awake all night, looking out the window into the darkness. I tell one of the guards to get the nurses. They know about Cinda and will get permission from the doctor to give her a shot of Haldol in her ass. That usually fixes this shit. It will knock her right out and maybe she'll forget all about the damn geese and predators.

But the guard tells me to shut up and mind my own business. "Who died and made you the doctor?" She sneers at me and goes back to her copy of *People* magazine.

Most days I'd use the rude comment as an excuse to fight. But this time, I let it go. In a way, I admire Cinda's half-crazed vigil. For whatever reason, she cares about the geese and has made a commitment to protect them. Even if no one cares about her (which is the truth), she still cares about someone else, if you can call a goose a someone.

I had someone to care about. Jasmine. And I messed it up. Maybe the truth is that what I really want is someone to care about me. Is that too much to ask for?

32

Cinda spotted a red fox this morning. It loped out of the woods at the edge of the parking lot. She said it trotted by the pond and then vanished back into the underbrush. She waited for Cyrus to come on shift and then pumped him for information about foxes. Cyrus told her what he knew, which was considerable. He said the fox was probably either starving or sick. Otherwise, it would never have come so close to humans. Cyrus said there were too many deterrents for a healthy fox to come near: garbage, exhaust fumes, the smell of food from the kitchen. These were all things linked to humans, and foxes fear humans.

Cyrus said that the fox would have a difficult time getting past the male goose. The goose would hover off the ground, flap his wings madly, hiss, and jab at the fox with his beak. The goose would then position himself directly between the attacker and the nesting female. A smart fox would turn away, Cyrus said.

The real danger, however, lies in the weeks immediately after hatching. The tiny goslings will trail behind their parents in a line. On land, or close enough to shore, a fox could make a mad dash and snatch one. If it's successful, it could keep snatching them until they're all gone.

I can see the wheels turning in Cinda's head. The babies haven't even hatched yet and the predators are lining up. It's too similar to Cinda's life, or mine, for that matter. The foxes are the pimps. "Hey, shorty, you too fine to be all by yourself, without no man to buy you the nice things you deserve." "Damn, baby, what's it gonna take for me to get a piece of that ass?" "You got to come work for me. I'll treat you so nice." The dog packs are the johns or tricks. "I'm so hungry." "Give it to me." "I want . . ." And the hawks and vultures are the rapists and child molesters. "I will take what I want. I want you. So I will take you."

I can see that Cinda is setting herself up for disaster. She knows the odds, can see how it will end. And still she's counting on a different ending. Counting on her ability to force a different outcome. She says, "I won't let anything get to them, Shavonne. I won't allow it."

I say, "How the hell are you gonna protect those geese, Cinda?"

"I don't know yet. But I'll figure it out. They need me."

And there you have it. The geese need her. Shit. That's exactly why I don't let myself have fantasies about my daughter needing me. It's Cinda's need. It's my own need. I'm not fooling anybody.

33

I can't watch my back all the time. I try, but then danger comes from so many different directions and takes different shapes. Today it comes in the form of Ms. Choi.

She has real power for a guard. You can see this in the way other guards kiss her fat ass: buy her sodas, ask her permission to go on break, shit like that. Even the administrators leave her alone—not because they can't squash her with absolute power or rank. They can. But they don't because she's a life-sucker. Going head to head with Ms. Choi is like tangling with a big cactus. Whatever you might do to her, she'll get you back ten times worse because she's that much meaner.

Physically, Ms. Choi is fat and disgusting. She wears her black hair in cornrows so tight they pull her eyebrows up. She drives a Lincoln Town Car with custom plates that say CHOI-GRL. No one knows how she got the Chinese name, because she's Caucasian, even though she talks like she's black.

On her face is a constant glare, and she seethes hatred from strange green eyes. The color itself is beautiful, but that's only if you can think of them apart from the rest of the package. The hate that comes out of those eyes almost makes my own seem trivial. It's a hate that takes delight in others' pain.

"You think you're so damn smart, don't you?"

"Excuse me, Ms. Choi?"

It's shift change, and the three-to-eleven staff are coming in. Choi heads straight for me, finger pointing, green eyes blazing. I have no idea what I've done to make her mad.

"Don't give me that shit, Shavonne. You know exactly what I'm talking about, right?"

"No, Ms. Choi. I don't know what you're talking about."

"See? That's just the kind of answer a smart pretty girl like you would give, isn't it? Covering all the bases, Shavonne. That's what you do best, right? Plot, scheme, set people up? Well, I can set people up too. You just wait and see, little girl."

She sneers this last part and makes it sound ugly. Kiki leans over and says, "Don't sweat it, girl, she just be trippin'." Kiki is plump, voluptuous. She works furiously at her long thin braids, holding pieces of weave in her mouth. Very quietly, so only I can hear she says, "That bitch is so fat and ugly and mean, she can't keep no man around. She just broke up with Kowalski because she found out he's

105

been fuckin' one of the girls on the overnight shift. You wasn't doin' him, was you? Maybe that's why she be raggin' on you."

I whisper back, "No, never. All I know about that man is that he restrained Samantha."

"Well, it don't matter. He just some big dummy. Double dummy. First, he stupid and blind enough to go with that pig. Second, he stupid enough to start givin' it to one of them new girls up on the beginner unit. Fool, thinkin' that nobody'll find out. Girl, you should *know* this! You always know what's goin' on. What's up with you?"

"I don't know, Kiki. I haven't been paying attention."

"Shoot. I know that's true because you involved in this shit! They only found out because of that story you told about gettin' pregnant! Mr. Slater went and interviewed all the male guards who could have been with you. Tyreena was waitin' outside Slater's office to clean. You *know* that girl can clean! You know she like to clean so much that—"

"Kiki, get to the point. Did Tyreena hear something?"

"Oh yeah, I almost forgot. She heard the big dummy break down crying. He spilled the whole story 'bout cheatin' on Choi with a resident. Said it wasn't his fault. Said the girl came on to him! I can't believe you didn't know, Shavonne. You usually down with everything."

I thank Kiki for the info. It all makes sense. No wonder Choi is out to get me: my lies fucked up her situation. In her mind, I'm to blame for losing her man. Jesus, what a mess. I need time to figure out how to deal with this woman before she gets to me first.

34

The retarded girl, Mary, is ready to burst. It turns out that she's almost eight months pregnant. She's got that dark line down her belly and her navel is pushed out. The baby kicks all the time and she lets us feel it.

She won't talk about the baby's father. That means one of two things: either she was raped, or she went along with it but the guy's old as hell. I know the female guards here would say, "Honey, they both the same thing." But they're not. Ask any fifteen-year-old girl at the Center how old her last boyfriend was. She'll say twenty or twenty-five or even thirty years old. It's not right or wrong. It's just how it is.

My mom was sixteen when she had me. Guess how old my father was? Thirty. Almost twice her age. That's why Mary's not talking about it. Whenever someone asks her, she just flashes that dumb smile and looks down at her feet, or her belly, or someplace far away. Who knows where.

Those of us with children of our own avoid Mary. We don't want to think about it, our babies at home being raised by our mothers and grandmothers or even by strangers. But really we avoid Mary because we know what's going to happen to her. We can practically feel the Social Services people closing in, old women in panty hose and those starchy skirts, all the cheap perfume to cover up the cigarette smoke from their hurried breaks outside in the cold.

Maybe this girl, Mary, can't take care of her kid. But it sucks. How'd she get pregnant in the first place? Who was watching out for her? Who was protecting her? Everyone's willing to step up and take care of her innocent little baby, but what about an innocent fourteen-year-old retarded girl who doesn't know who to trust?

This is why I stay away from Mary and others like her. The sad sacks. The helpless. The misfits and fuck-ups. Mary, Cinda, and all the others. They're not like Tyreena and Kiki, who know how to protect themselves. They're tough, so nobody's going to hurt them. I wish I could be like that.

35

Today I get to leave the facility for a med trip. Cinda and three other girls have cavities; I need to have my front teeth capped. No dentist will come to the facility, so we have to drive twenty miles to the nearest city.

As much as I hate dentists, I am eager to get out. Don't get me wrong; riding in a state van with shackles on your hands and feet is not my idea of fun, but it's a break from the facility.

And there is cool stuff to see. Cyrus, who is driving the van, points out red-tailed hawks and a bunch of deer. And for the first time I get to see Amish people. There's this buggy pulled by a horse. It's moving real slowly on the side of the road: a black horse pulling a plain black carriage with that bright orange triangle nailed to it. Cinda and I stare into the carriage to see the family inside. There's a father, with one of those Abe Lincoln beards. He's wearing a black hat. Next to him sits his wife. She's wearing a white bonnet and is very plain-looking. Behind them you can see the heads of two or three small children. They look so comfortable, bundled up together under warm blankets.

Then we drive by this farm. It has a battered old house surrounded by fields. Cyrus slows the van and points to an Amish guy. He is plowing the field with a big brown horse. He wears suspenders and a straw hat and rides a kind of old-fashioned plow I've never seen before. They move slow and steady, the point of the plow digging into the dirt.

It is really quite a scene. The sun hangs just above the distant trees, making the whole field glow. And in the center of this soft orange light is an old-fashioned man and his horse. It's like the world or the earth or whatever is so pleased with this scene that it can't help but draw attention and point it out to us. "Look," it says, "because there's still wonder."

Cinda starts giggling in delight. The other girls laugh outright and say that it's mad corny. I don't know how to explain my own feelings. A warmth surges up inside me, like I'm seeing something really important and powerful, and it doesn't even matter if I understand it; it's enough just to be here and look. It's so strange, but I don't want the moment to be broken by words.

It's like sneaking up on something very special that isn't meant for you, like getting lost in the woods and finding a fawn taking its first steps. Does that sound corny? I don't care if it does. I've never seen anything like that before, but I always wanted to. That Amish farmer isn't doing anything to impress anyone. He isn't fronting or putting on a show; he's just doing his regular work like he's done every day since he was a boy. But he fits in perfectly, with the horse and the field and the glowing sun around him. It is so beautiful, though I can't really explain why.

Then Cinda breaks the spell and starts asking questions. "Cyrus, what kind of horse is that? How does the plow stay straight? Why not use a tractor—is the man too poor to afford one?" Most of the questions are legitimate, but some are ridiculous. "Cyrus, that horse is pretty big. How long do you think its penis is?"

She laughs, that crazy energy building up inside her. She turns freakish, obsessing about the horse's genitals, making up songs where she rhymes "Niagara Falls" with "horse's balls." I tell her to shut up, because she's getting on everyone's nerves and Cyrus is having a hard time driving. The other guard in the front seat keeps whispering to him about what to do. But there isn't anything to do. Either she shuts up or she doesn't. She isn't reasonable or logical, and I don't think the guards ever really get it. Crazy is just plain crazy. You can't make sense of it.

Cinda listens to me and, for the most part, quiets down. If you don't know her, you'd think she's a cute kid. Even though she's seventeen, she looks only about twelve or thirteen. She has this short sandy-colored hair and the palest blue eyes. Almost gray. Her skin is very pink and she blushes easily. She's bone thin and has no breasts. It's like she skipped puberty and decided to stay a little girl.

But not really, because she is always making bizarre sexual comments to people.

I think that's what freaks everyone out so much about Cinda, this split between what she looks like on the outside and how she really is. Sometimes, at least. That's why the guards are afraid of her. This wispy seventeen-year-old with the chopped-up hair and pale blue eyes actually scares people.

I have to admit that sometimes she scares me. Like this one time when I caught her watching me sleep. But most of the time I think she's just sad and pathetic. She was abused like the rest of us, but in her case it broke her mind. One minute she's okay, then the next she's screaming, crying, saying bizarre things. Sometimes she needs to go to the hospital, but they rarely keep her for long. She masturbates constantly, and wets the bed unless she takes special pills. Sometimes she refuses her meds and gets really out of control.

In the van, Cinda is quiet, staring out the window. I forget about her and talk to Cyrus. He tells me more about the Amish, how they live the way people did hundreds of years ago. He says they make their own clothes, grow their own food, teach their children in their own schools. They don't trust outsiders and take care of each other in ways we couldn't understand.

I get so wrapped up in Cyrus's talk and my own thoughts that I don't notice Cinda. Her shackles have been rattling for several minutes, ever since we passed a burned-up old house with melted garbage in the front yard. Her cuffs rattle insanely, but I just figure she's playing with her-self again. And who could blame me for not wanting to deal with that? I slide away from her on the vinyl bench seat, at least as far as the shackles will allow.

But something is wrong, I think, because it's too quiet. Cinda is staring out the window with a blank look. Her eyes are dead, vacant. Her hands rest palms-up on her lap. The left wrist is sliced open along the veins. It's an ugly jagged cut, made from the edge of an ashtray lid. It looks like she pried the lid off the armrest and cut the hell out of herself with it. The blood is bright red, spurting out of the wound. It makes dripping noises on the plastic floor mats.

There's a moment when my heart stops cold. I have the feeling like the whole world is ending. Like I'm going to die, which doesn't make any sense. Cinda's the one who's bleeding. My sneaker slides on the warm blood. All I can think of is getting it off my shoe. I don't want to touch it. It's slippery now but will soon turn sticky.

As best I can, dealing with my own cuffs and Cinda's, I grab hold of Cinda's wrist and clamp my hand down over the wound. She doesn't seem to notice and continues to stare blankly out the window. I choke back tears and try to sound calm, but my voice is panicked, screeching. "Cyrus, Cinda's bleeding. We gotta go to the hospital. It's bad."

Without hesitating, Cyrus pulls over to have a look. The other guard is useless. Cyrus takes off his jacket and stuffs it through the gap between the top of the cage and the van's roof. It gets stuck and I have trouble pulling it the rest of the way through because my hands are shaking so bad. Cyrus says, "Wrap it as tight as you can around the cut and then squeeze it hard with both your hands. Don't let go until we get to the hospital and the doctors tell you to back off. Talk to her, Shavonne. Tell her nice things and don't stop talking."

Then he says to the other guard, "Get your ass back there and help." The guard asks what to do. "I don't give a shit!" Cyrus says. "Just get back there and help in some way. Talk to the girls, tell them it'll be okay. Take off your goddamn jacket and put it around Cinda. She's probably in shock." Cyrus is clearly losing his temper, but he's still in control. I've never seen him like this, but I'm glad he's the one in charge.

My hands are squeezing the jacket around the wound. I feel sick, like I might throw up. This girl's life, her blood, is soaking through the jacket and coating my hands. It's warm and slick. I feel the rhythm and also the pressure of the flow. It's my job to keep that force from spilling completely out of her.

"Cyrus, my hands are covered in blood. There's so much blood. I can't do this." I have to get out of here. I can't do this. It's too fucked up. It reminds me of something bad, but I can't remember what. Don't want to remember.

"That's okay, Shavonne. You're doing a good job. Just keep squeezing. She'll be okay."

I pray for the second time this month. *Please God, don't*

let this girl die. Don't let her die. I also pray to be taken away from this.

Then this last thought takes hold. It's a selfish thought, but I can't drive it away. *Run.* First chance I get, I will run and get the fuck away. This is what I think, because I am a schemer; I am a selfish, heartless taker.

At the hospital I will go to the bathroom to wash off the blood. It has to be a bathroom on the perimeter, one with a window. Climb out and run. Break into a nearby house that's empty and get some real clothes. Hitch a ride out of town. Get away from all this. It's too much.

But then the impulse to run fades as quickly as it came. There is no way I'm letting go of Cinda until the doctors are on the scene. And then I will want to know her condition. If it looks like she's going to die, then I'll run. This is a better plan.

The other guard, Grinnel, gets into the back. He looks scared and nervous and is no help at all. He keeps looking at the blood on my hands, my clothes, and the floor. Then he looks at Cinda and he gags, but at least he doesn't vomit. The other girls watch in horror.

36

After the nightmare of Cinda's suicide attempt, I crash in my bed for twelve hours straight. But instead of feeling refreshed, I awaken with a sense of dread . . . like the med trip is just the beginning of a series of bad things, like the dam's broken and there's no holding it back.

Sure enough, when I press my face against the windowpane, I can see that the nest is littered with downy feathers and shards of eggshells. It looks like it's been ransacked or trampled. And I can't help but think that it's somehow connected to Cinda, like her watchfulness at the window is what really kept the predators at bay. I should probably feel sad or something, but I'm just numb because too much crazy stuff is happening. Cinda almost killed herself. The goslings are dead. The only question is, What, or who, is next?

Delpopolo knocks on my door and asks if we can talk

in the unit lounge. This is kind of strange since I always see him in his office.

"Shavonne, I heard about Cinda. I'm sorry you had to go through that, but I understand you did a remarkable job."

"Yeah. Have you heard anything about her? Is she okay?"

"Well, she's not okay, but she'll survive, if that's what you mean."

"Mr. D, do you know why she did that?"

"Yes. There are rules about situations like this, but you've become as involved as anybody else. And for that you deserve to know why."

Delpopolo tells me Cinda's story. The parts he leaves out I fill in with guesses and some things Cinda told me before. Cinda is local. Most of the girls here are from big cities, hundreds of miles away. But Cinda's from a shitty little farmhouse not twenty miles east.

Her father was a child molester. He molested kids in the neighborhood and also his two daughters. The family kept the secret until the eighth grade, when Cinda made a suicide attempt and was sent away to a psychiatric hospital. The hospital called Child Protective Services, and a restraining order was filed against the father, ordering him away from his house and his daughters. That night, he snuck into his old neighborhood, poured gas all around the perimeter of the house, and torched it while his wife and one daughter slept. Then he shot himself in the front yard. Only Cinda survived.

Incredibly, the guards at the Center didn't know the story. Maybe they never read the newspaper. I don't know. But Cyrus drove Cinda right through her hometown and past the burned-out house where her family died. That's what set her off. *Can you imagine seeing that?*

Delpopolo says I saved her life. I snap back, "I saved her life for what? So she can spend it in mental hospitals without a family? I'm not so sure I did her a favor."

"Maybe, but that's not for you to decide."

I know Mr. D is trying to be decent, and I'm sorry I answered in such a sarcastic way, but it's how I feel. The whole thing is so horrible I can't talk to anyone about it. Cyrus is still at the hospital and the other guard quit. So no one really knows what happened or what it was like for me.

At one point, before I wrapped Cyrus's jacket around the wound, I felt something like one of Cinda's tendons pop up through the opening. How do I make that memory go away?

Then Delpopolo hits me with a question out of left field.

"Since we're talking about suicide, why haven't you killed yourself?"

I just stare at him. "Whose side are you on, Mr. D? If you want to get rid of me, just say so."

"I don't mean that. What I mean is that you've got a good point. Some people have lives that are so bad death seems like a good way out. You ever think that way?"

"Yes."

"And how is it that you're still here? Why didn't you go through with it?"

"I tried, a bunch of times, but I always screwed it up."

"Yes, but you're very smart and very determined. I'll bet that if you really wanted to, no one could stop you. You'd find a way."

"Yeah, you're right about that. I know lots of ways."

"So answer the question, Shavonne. Why do you choose to stick around? Do you have some plans for yourself?"

37

Mr. Slater, the director, comes to see me today during dinner. I know he doesn't like me, but today he's all smiles and shakes my hand.

"We're very proud of you, Shavonne. You did a good thing, and we're in your debt."

"Thanks." The silence between us is uncomfortable.

"I'll get right to the point, Shavonne. Your record here is terrible. Before that incident with Cinda, you were working on a one-way pass to adult corrections on your eighteenth birthday. Did you know that? It doesn't matter, though, because things are different now."

Then he tells me the deal. I have to keep my nose clean for one month. That means no fights, no restraints, no stealing sandwiches, etc. And—this is the important part—if outsiders come in to ask questions about "the incident," I have to "emphasize the safety precautions that were already in place, as well as the positive manner in which the guards responded." In other words, I have to downplay some of the fuck-ups that occurred. Slater is very careful with his words.

"Mr. Slater, I want to say something, if it's okay."

"Sure, go ahead." Shifting on his feet, looking at his watch, wanting to leave.

"I know how my record looks to other people. I can't convince you that I've changed, but I want you to know I'm tired of fighting everything and everybody, and I want to leave. I want to get my life back. I want to see my daughter again."

Mr. Slater gets up and straightens his suit, offers his hand once again. "We'll see what we can do, young lady. I expect some people will be coming by to talk to you about the incident later this week. You comfortable with that?"

"Yes, sir."

"Gooood." He flashes that incredible smile as he drags the word "good" out a second too long. He's basically saying, "I'll be watching you, kid. Don't fuck this up or it'll be bad for you." And I believe him.

38

Back with Delpopolo, I tell him about my plan. I want to get out of here and go to a mother-daughter group home. I'll get Jasmine back, and work on a job and an apartment. With luck, Slater will keep his deal and send word to set me loose.

What I don't tell Mr. D is that Slater will never keep his word and I'll have to force the whole damn thing in court: refuse to sign the petition for an extension of placement, tell the judge all about Cinda's "accident," Kowalski screwing one of the girls, other stuff. The judge will call Slater to investigate and he'll say, "Cut her loose. Too much trouble."

Delpopolo says, "I admire your plan, Shavonne. But if it's going to work, it's got to seem real to you. Right now it's too far away, and I'm afraid you're caught up in schemes and plots and drama. I'm afraid that you're trying to control things that are really outside of your control."

It's like he can read my mind.

"How do you know I'm scheming?"

"Because it's your job. You're supposed to try to avoid doing the hard work. It's what I'd do if I were in your shoes."

"But then what's wrong with it?"

"It won't work. You can't control it. Haven't you noticed that this place is part of a system? And you can't go up against a system. It won't budge for you."

39

Today after dinner Ms. Stokes, the cottage leader, calls me into her office. I think maybe I'm in trouble. Ms. Stokes is a small black woman with short hair. She wears African robes and jewelry: jade, turquoise, bone, silver. She is really beautiful and carries herself with what I can only think of as grace.

I haven't mentioned her till now because she's scarce. She's hardly ever at the cottage. I think she spends her time at meetings. And she supervises the guards. I hear them mumbling about her sometimes. But it is never anything real bad, because Ms. Stokes is what you'd call professional. She is fair and strict and has the respect of almost everybody, kids and guards alike.

"Have a seat, Shavonne."

My gut instinct is to stay standing and say something smart like "No thanks." But I sit and fold my hands in my lap. Ms. Stokes has on bifocals and is reading some official-looking piece of paper.

Still staring at the paper, she says, "You were a real hero the other day. Whether or not it means anything to you, I'm proud, Shavonne. Not many people can react that way under pressure. It says a lot about your heart."

"Thanks, Ms. Stokes."

"Cinda probably won't be coming back. You know that?"

"I figured." I continue to look down at my hands.

Ms. Stokes looks up from her paper, staring me in the eye, forcing me to look up at her.

"Shavonne, you know you'll have to get a new room-mate."

I don't say anything. I know where this is going. A ton of shit is about to fall right on my head in the form of Mary, the retarded pregnant girl. Mary's single room is getting turned into a new staff office. She's going to have to move in with someone. Guess who that's going to be!

"You'll be sharing a room with Mary. You know her? Of course you do. Listen, Shavonne, this girl needs some-one to help her out a little bit." Ms. Stokes leans toward me and places a hand on my knee. "I know you want to be left alone to take care of yourself, but you're the only one on the whole unit right now who I can trust with this."

"Trust?" I nearly scream. "You trust me? I'm locked up. I have no rights. I could get transferred to adult prison on my birthday. I can't be trusted, Ms. Stokes. You *know* that."

I don't even know if this is sarcastic or true—I just don't want to be responsible for that girl.

She raises her voice a notch. "Shavonne, you don't decide who I do and do not trust."

I feel bone tired. I don't want to talk or think or feel. I don't want anyone to raise their voice and look me in the eye. I want to say, "Ms. Stokes, I admire you in a certain way because you're a strong and competent woman, but you don't know me! If you did, you wouldn't be having this conversation with me right now. You'd leave me the fuck alone and stick that kid with someone else."

Ms. Stokes continues quietly and slowly. "I trust you with this responsibility. You just saved a girl's life! I've never saved anybody's life. You want to trivialize that, go ahead. But I will not. I *am* proud of you, Shavonne. And I'm sure you'll be a good roommate for Mary."

I remain silent but scream inside. *You bitch! Do you have any idea what that simpleminded girl and her baby can do to me? My heart can't break again. It will kill me. I'd rather room with Ms. Choi!*

40

Mary spends a lot of time trying to fold her clothes like they do at the Gap, where everything is neat and organized. She's not very good at it, but I know just what she's trying to do. Because I'm the same way. The dirtier the life, the more effort you put into keeping things clean and organized. Just walk into some shitty apartment in the projects with plastic covers on the furniture. It will reek of Carpet Fresh and Lysol. Roach traps everywhere and that blue stuff that goes in the toilet bowl to make it look like a bathroom in a cheap hotel. And all the family members will be frozen forever on the walls in black lacquer picture frames. Their beautiful smiles and fancy clothes almost convince you that they have happy and complete lives. In actuality, though, some are dead, while the rest are in jail for armed robbery, attempted murder, or drugs.

When Mary finishes organizing, she sits on the edge of

her bed with her legs dangling over. She puts her hands on her belly. She smiles. It's a stupid smile, but happy. How can she be happy? She's fourteen years old and about to have a baby. I could tell her a few things, but what's the point? If she's really happy, then who am I to ruin it? She looks my way and starts talking.

"I'm Mary." Again with the smile. I just stare at her. Is she for real?

"I know."

"I guess we're gonna be roommates."

"Right."

"Do you—"

I interrupt. "Listen, Mary. I don't know if I'd be such a good friend for you right now. I've got my own problems and I need to keep to myself. Understand?"

She stops talking instantly, nods. Then she puts her hands back on her tummy and kicks her legs back and forth. When I forget about her she talks again.

"Sorry, Shavonne. I won't bother you no more." She is crying. Against my better judgment, I go over and sit on the bed next to her. Mary smiles and dries her tears.

"Do you want to feel the baby kick?" she asks. I do.

"His name is Ramón, after my papa."

41

Mary moves around a lot in her sleep. She thrashes and kicks the bedding onto the floor. Sometimes, half awake from a bad dream, she clamps her legs shut and covers her privates with her hands shouting out, "No. No. I don't want to. Please!" It doesn't take a psychologist to figure out what's going on here.

But in the morning, she's right as rain, smiling her dumb smile and trying to be so nice and friendly. "Hi, Shavonne," she says. *Hi, Mary.*

That's about the extent of our conversations. Whenever I feel her looking for an opening to talk, I grab a book and bury my face in it. She takes the hint and continues staring out the window.

Then I feel guilty again and I sit by her. We play Uno even though she doesn't really understand all the rules. Sometimes I let her win. One day she gets a box of home-made cookies in the mail and shares them with me.

"These are from my auntie," she says. "She's mad pretty like you. I told her all about you. She says you're nice for helping me. I know I need help, Shavonne. I ain't stupid, you know. I'm just a little slow because I don't know no numbers or how to tell time and stuff. But my auntie says that's okay, because everyone needs help sometimes, right?"

I tell her that her auntie is a smart lady. I tell her everything is going to be okay with her baby and she'll get out of here soon. I tell her whatever she wants to hear because it's not much when you think about it. It doesn't take a lot of work to reassure a nice person like Mary. Even if no one can do it for me, it's a small effort and it makes me feel good to see her beautiful innocent smile.

42

Today Cinda calls. She says the hospital is great. "People are so nice here, Shavonne," she says. "There's this boy. We've got so much in common, Shavonne. He tried to kill himself too! You'd really like him, I know you would." I play along. Why the hell not? Why shouldn't these two people on the edge of insanity and suicide find comfort in each other?

Cinda changes the subject. "Shavonne, what happened to the geese? Are they okay? You didn't let anything happen to them, did you?"

I nearly drop the phone, even though I knew she'd ask. What am I supposed to do: be honest with her and risk her having another breakdown? I lie and tell her the eggs haven't hatched yet. I think she believes me, but she sounds worried.

"They should have hatched by now. Promise me, Shavonne, that you'll keep an eye on them and protect them. It's up to you to make sure that they're okay. I got to go. Love you. Bye!"

She hangs up and is gone. For some reason, I don't think I'll ever hear from her again. And this makes me sad. I'm afraid for her because she's so fragile. I'm afraid that the world just doesn't accept fragile people like Cinda and Mary. It chews them up or squashes them into the ground.

43

My hair is beginning to fall out in clumps. My mind races all day and half the night. I try to go over all the things I'm supposed to do to get out of here, but mostly I cook up scenarios where everything goes bad.

Tonight, though, I think about Cinda's geese. Is there any chance that they're alive? Maybe some of them made it. Or am I just being stupid and naive? Cyrus will know. Tomorrow I'll ask him.

Before drifting off, I think about Jasmine. Does she remember me? Does she think about me, or is the foster mother the only "mommy" she knows?

Then I wonder about my mother. I try to picture her in a nice way, in a motherly way, but I can't. Too much has happened. The memories start out with us taking a walk to a park or the basketball courts, but then she leaves me with somebody. Leaves me with strangers. "I'll be back, baby. Don't get in no trouble." That's what she'd say when she'd go off to get high. Did she ever love me? Or was I an afterthought, something to get rid of? I don't think she liked me. Maybe I wasn't likable. Probably I wasn't.

44

At dawn, I get up and look across the bedroom toward the window. Prints of Cinda's fingers and nose remain on the glass. Ghost prints. Smudged reminders of her. I'm tempted to look for the geese, just in case it was a mistake, like maybe they just hatched and are running around out there.

But I decide that I won't ask Cyrus about the geese because I can't bear the answer. Not that I care so much about the actual birds. It's more like I care about what they represent. Like the canaries or pigeons I read about that miners used to send down into the shafts. If the birds stayed alive, it meant the air was okay.

I think the fate of Mary's baby is tied to the fate of the hatchlings. Because if a bunch of fucking bird eggs can't survive in this stinking place, then how will a baby? And if Mary's baby doesn't survive, then what chance do the rest of us girls have?

It's a messed-up way to think, I know. But I can't stop. I look again toward the window and imagine that, below, coyotes and foxes are feasting on eggs and feathers. A shiver runs through me because of what might be out there. Plus it's so damn cold. It makes me think that nothing can survive for long here.

I am becoming superstitious. I look for signs in everything. Hawks, crows, and foxes are all death signs. Mary's big belly should be a sign of birth, life, or beauty, but it's not. Instead it's a sign of disaster. Birth defects, stillbirth, foster care. Where are the good signs? Where is something beautiful? I really need something beautiful right now.

45

It's the three-to-eleven shift and Ms. Choi is glaring at me. She came in messed-up-looking, like she hadn't slept or showered, bags under her eyes, shirt untucked. Whenever she bends over or reaches for something, the shirt rides up, showing the tattoo on the small of her back. It says *Tony* in dark green letters. She's got stretch marks on the fat around her waist. I now know that Tony is the name of the guard she's been screwing. Tony Kowalski. Some name.

Things aren't looking good for me on this shift. The two guards are Choi and Ms. Williams. It's Ms. Williams's first shift back since the sandwich incident. She ignores me for a while, then calls me into the staff office. She's jumpy and nervous, like just the sight of me makes her upset.

"You sit there and listen and don't say a word. Don't

you dare try to apologize 'cause I don't want it. If you understand me, you can nod."

Her voice cracks at this last part. I nod. I am ashamed. I hate myself and that makes me angry, but this talk is not really for me. It's for her, so she can get back to her work and put it behind her. This is fair. More than fair. So I look down at my feet to make it easier for Ms. Williams to talk. She starts to get her rhythm. Her voice becomes stronger.

"I know you got problems, Shavonne, but I don't give a damn no more. You're on your own. You wanna hate people who got nothin' to do with the reasons you're messed up? Go ahead. But keep your fuckin' hands off me and the people I work with. You do whatever the hell you want when you leave the Center. But while you're here, stay out of my way and don't ask me for nothin'. If I tell you to do somethin', all I want to hear from you is 'Yes, Ms. Williams.' "

She stops talking and I say, "Yes, Ms. Williams." I move toward the door with my head down.

"Sit down, girl! I ain't through yet." In a panicked tone now, eyes watery, losing control. "Shavonne, I helped deliver your baby! I was there, remember? I was there when she came into this world and took her first breath. And I was there when the nurses took her away from you and it looked like your soul broke in two. Remember? And I cried with you, Shavonne, and I prayed for you every day. Did you know that? Every day I said a prayer for you and your baby."

She pauses and looks out the window. I can't tell if she's

still crying. I make a decision: if she hits me, I'm not going to fight back. I'm not going to press charges, either. I will give up control, like Delpopolo says.

"I never expected nothin' in return 'cause I thought it was my responsibility as a woman to the next generation of women. But you gave me somethin' back, Shavonne. You gave me a black eye, a concussion, and two loose teeth. That's what I got for bein' there for you. So fuck you! You hurt people and don't even care. What kind of person does that? A psycho. A person with no feelings. A taker. Go. Get out of here!"

I stagger out of the office like I've been beaten with something heavy. Everything Ms. Williams said is true. If she hurt me, then it was with truth. She was there for me when I really needed somebody. I had never even asked for her help. She just knew. In my worst moment, when they took my baby, she was there. Not my mother. Not my father. It had only been Ms. Williams.

Am I a taker? Do I have no feelings? What does sorry feel like, anyway? What's it supposed to feel like? I don't know. I know when I'm *supposed to* feel sorry. Then it gets twisted up inside of me and I think, *I'm supposed to be sorry? Well, fuck that! Fuck you if you think I'm going to feel sorry for you.*

On the unit, everyone is looking at me. Most of the girls like Ms. Williams. She shares her books, braids our hair, and rents cool movies for us to watch. The girls liked the distraction of the fight, too, but now they are righteous and outraged, thinking about all the nice things Ms.

Williams does for them. They glare and suck their teeth. If there were a pile of stones nearby I'd get blasted. I'd be covered with welts in a heartbeat.

But there's a different kind of punishment waiting for me in the form of Ms. Choi. I clear my head of this business with Ms. Williams, because I need to pay attention. I need to stay on my toes.

46

"What about your father, Shavonne?" Delpopolo is grim.

"What about him?" I've learned Delpopolo's trick of answering a question with a question.

"Is he alive?"

"No. And I don't want to talk about him."

"Why?"

"Because I don't think about him. So why should I talk about him? Just because you want me to?"

"Did he hurt you?"

"He wasn't around enough to hurt me. He was never around. Never. Not ever."

I wait for the next question, but Mr. D sits there like a stone, looking at me, hands in his lap. I get the idea. He wants me to talk about how it all makes me feel. Shrink bullshit. I go mute and we sit, each refusing to speak. It is uncomfortable. I want to stop playing games. I am tired of games, even my own.

After a few minutes I talk. I just don't give a shit anymore. He wants me to talk, I'll talk.

"He was in jail when I was born. Drugs, I think. Other stuff too, I'm sure. But nobody tells me."

Delpopolo nods and plays with his fountain pen. It's a nice one: real silver with delicate filigree. He offers it to me and I take it. I've never held one before, and the ink flows out smoothly as I sketch how I think my father would look if he were alive. The eyes come out hard and mean-looking, which doesn't fit with my memory. I keep talking. The words spill out and I listen to them as though they belong to someone else.

"He used to write me letters from prison. They were nice letters too. He called me Princess and Sweet Pea. It made me feel good at the time, because I was living in a foster home. I had this fantasy that my daddy would come and rescue me. Every night I imagined him kicking the living shit out of my foster mother's boyfriend. Then he'd take me away and we'd live happily ever after."

"Didn't happen?"

"No. He got sick in prison and died before he ever got paroled. Liver disease or something. He never rescued me."

I scratch out the picture of my father and move on to a profile of Mary with her bulging belly. I'm talking easily now. I am telling my story, the story of how I came to be this way: a messed-up, ungrateful person. A taker. A person without feelings. I tell Delpopolo this is how I feel.

Delpopolo says, "It's not so. You're numb, and that's different from having no feelings. Kids your age only go numb because they have to—when that's the only thing that makes sense.

"When a life becomes unlivable," he says, "you *have* to go numb."

"Then how do I get better? How do I change?"

"By talking and feeling. And thinking. You're doing a fine job of that right now. Please, go on."

But I've run out of words, and images. I give him back his fountain pen.

47

Ms. Choi glares at me with evil crazy eyes. She's made a half-assed attempt to put herself together, but the effect is grotesque: lipstick and mascara applied in thick uneven strokes. Maybe her hand is unsteady from drinking or not sleeping. I don't know. But she's staring at me, smiling. It's a predator's smile, like a hyena's. I saw a hyena at the zoo once. It had gone insane. Its pen was too small and it paced endlessly. Ms. Choi isn't doing anything like that. She sits perfectly still, but the grin is the same as the crazy hyena's.

She points to a desk chair in front of her and says, "Sit." I do as I'm told. Ms. Choi stands up, maybe expecting some kind of fight. She turns to the rest of the girls and addresses them.

"All of yous turn in and mind your own business. You all gonna get sore necks rubberneckin' like that!"

The girls roll their eyes and open their paperbacks from library class. They disappear into their romances, horror books, street stories. Ms. Choi leans over and whispers, "I got your number, Shavonne. You can expect it any day now. It's a fact."

48

Meal call is serious. Everybody is hungry and so we don't fuck around. Instead of teasing each other and complaining, we line up and wait to move. When the cue comes over the radio "Unit cleared to move to cafeteria," a guard says, "Go on, move!" and we all start walking.

In the Center, you always have a specific place in line. I'm number eleven, so I fall in behind number ten, Kiki. Mary is number twelve, so she stands behind me. Only, today, Ms. Choi puts her hand on Mary's shoulder and says, "You're going to be number fifteen today, dear."

Number fifteen, Edna, is a chubby girl with a wild Afro that sticks straight up in the air. Edna is strange. She talks so fast that no one can understand her. She moves near Mary and starts dancing in place, snapping her fingers, waiting for Mary to move.

None of this is unusual. Guards switch us around all the time if we're arguing or talking. Edna knows this and is simply entertaining herself while waiting. She doesn't see or notice the scared look on Mary's face, but I do. I know that she is having trouble doing the math of the switch, subtracting twelve from fifteen, then counting off by that number from her present position. So she just stands there, immobile, looking like a statue of a fourteen-year-old pregnant retarded girl who is confused and scared.

Ms. Choi is staring at me. I see now what's going on, how she's working on Mary, my new roommate, thinking it will get to me. I twitch, trying to keep the rage inside me, but Choi breathes in my anxiety like a snake tasting the air. She's set this whole thing up perfectly. It's her disgusting masterpiece.

She takes a few steps back. Her eyes stay fixed on me because she's not taking any chances. A couple of guards, big boys with thumbs looped in their thick black leather belts, lurk down the hallway. They've got Choi's back.

"Mary, honey." She is being oh so sweet! "What's the problem? You have to change places in line with Edna so we can all go to dinner. Now move!"

Mary starts moving, then stops. She looks over at me for help, but I look away. All she has to do to break the spell is talk. She can say "I don't know where to go," or "I don't know how to subtract and then add," or "I'm confused." She can move back in line and slide in where number fourteen, Jovanna, and number sixteen, Christie, have already made space.

But the spell is strong and she continues to stand there. Choi's plan is a clever one. In a girl like Mary, confusion and embarrassment get manufactured into defiance. And defiance is all the fuel Ms. Choi needs to take this further.

"All right, Mary." The tone is different. There's an edge to it. No longer is it sugary sweet. "You're holdin' us up! Why? 'Cause you won't follow simple instructions. We'll just have to move you, then."

Choi nods to Ms. Swain, a short dumpy-looking white woman with a puckered face and bleached hair. Female guards are supposed to do the restraining whenever possible—too many lawsuits with the men. That's why Choi motions for Swain instead of one of the big boys, who I see moving closer. They're free to jump in if the women have any trouble.

Swain moves to grab one of Mary's arms. But as soon as she touches Mary, the spell breaks and the girl screams, "Don't touch me! Don't you touch me! Leave me alone!"

She's screaming and crying and completely out of control. It looks like her nightmares, only she's awake. She covers her face with her hands; her T-shirt rides up, showing her ripe belly. It's pathetic and we all know it. These guards are committing a terrible sin and they're making us all watch. No, it's worse than pathetic, because they're making us play a part.

The other girls are starting to get anxious. Some blame Mary and mutter things like "Dang, she mad stupid. Why don't she just do what she say and move?" Others side with Mary and say, "Jesus! Just leave her alone!" At this point, Choi pulls me out of line and turns me around to face the wall.

"You just stand there, girl! Don't look behind and don't say nothin'." I look at the wall and try hard to control my breathing. The spot on my upper arm where she touched me is burning. I want to smash her skull so badly, but I know she's counting on that. That's her plan: to get me pissed enough to attack. And she's just standing there, waiting, daring me to do it.

I try hard to picture my daughter's face smiling at me, but I can't. All I see is the face of Connie saying, "That's okay, Shavonne. Jasmine is fine with me. We love each other, right, Jasmine? She wants to stay with me, so you go ahead and beat this woman's ass. She deserves it. It's okay."

Now I can't see anything but the wall. I can hear Mary, though, cursing and struggling. What's happening? There are a couple of dull thuds. Are they really taking down a pregnant retarded girl?

"Mary!" I scream. I start to turn my head to see what's happening. The other girls are agitated too. Some are breathing quickly; others are crying and getting angry themselves. That's how it is: fear, helplessness, and rage all mix together until the whole thing blows, until the hearts and souls of these girls break apart into tiny pieces.

My body turns to follow my head. I get a glimpse of a pile of people on the floor. I see Mary, Swain, and the big boys. But where's Choi? I move closer to the struggling screaming mess of bodies on the floor. I can't see Mary. I hear her muffled screams, but I can't find her. Something heavy hits me in the back of my head and I black out.

49

In room confinement again, my head is pounding. Two nurses are there and they tell me I've got a concussion. "You need to take it easy, young lady."

The nurses are from a temp agency. The Center can't get any nurses to stay, so they hire whoever's available short-term. This means there's a steady stream of new nurses who really don't know us kids or even how things are supposed to be done. Which in a way means they're nice.

"Where's Mary?" I try to sit up but my head explodes with pain.

Rather than answer me, the two nurses give each other a look. It's not a good look, and the older one only answers when I try to get up again.

"She's at the emergency room. They just want to make sure her baby's okay. There was a lot of excitement today."

A lot of excitement? Is that what you call it? Excitement?

But I say nothing because it's all clear now. There's pay-back for everything, and I just got mine. Mary got hers, too, except she wasn't guilty of anything. They couldn't hurt me anymore, so they tied this other girl to me . . . made me feel the slightest bit responsible for her and then they hurt her. I tried my best to stay clear of Mary, but in the end, it didn't matter.

I cover my face with my hands and lie there for the rest of the day. I try not to think about Mary and her baby. She's got to be so scared. She won't understand what's happening or know what to do about it.

50

I return to my room high on Vicodin. My right eye is turning black and purple. One cheek is swollen, and the other has a rug burn that looks like raw meat. I run my fingers lightly over a puffy line on my chin; it has been closed up with stitches. I look at myself in the mirror and I look really bad.

Later, at my desk at school, I find an illiterate letter from Tyreena:

Yo, I ain't sayin I be ur friend or nothin', but that shit with Mary be fucked up! If u wanna get back at u know who, I help. Just give me them pills and I take care of the thing.

I shred the letter. It seems like a good plan, but I can't give her the pills. The nurses said they're a a narcotic and I can get a drug charge if I misuse them. Tyreena is looking at me, trying to get my attention. She mouths the words "You down?" I ignore her, knowing that this will earn me yet another enemy. Why not? Line 'em up.

In my room later, still high on painkillers, I look out the window constantly, even though I know they're gone. A floodlight shines bright on the empty nest. There's nothing left but bits of straw and some scattered feathers. Nothing good or new can survive in this place. Not the geese. Not Mary's baby. Not me.

51

Bad nightmares on the pills. In one dream my mother is having sex with a disgusting man. They're on a bed in a cheap motel and the man is doing her from behind. My mother's belly is huge because she's pregnant and it looks really creepy because the rest of her body is skinny. The man is banging away at her and she's laughing and talking dirty to him, but I can tell from the look on her face that she is not into it, she's just thinking about the crack she'll buy later.

I can see all this happening like I'm watching it on a TV screen. The bare mattress is stained with sweat and semen. I want to leave the room, but I can't because it occurs to me that the baby inside my mother is *me*. It's me inside her, and this awful man is trying to get at me. He's poking at me with his penis, and I see now that I've never been safe. Not even from the beginning. I never had a chance.

52

Delpopolo winces at the sight of my face. He says, "Who did this to you?"

"Ms. Choi."

"I heard about Mary, but I didn't know you were hurt as well. What happened?"

Delpopolo looks upset, but not with me. It's strange that he doesn't have all the information. I wonder why. Nothing seems to make sense.

"It's a long story and I'm tired. I've messed things up so bad, Mr. D. There's no way to fix it. It's over."

"You have a plan to get back at her?"

"Yeah. No. I mean, I did, but not anymore. I can think of a million reasons why that woman deserves to go down, but I just don't feel like doing it myself. It's like, I know I'm her enemy, but I don't know if she's mine."

He sits silent for a long time. Then he says, "I've got to make some phone calls, Shavonne. I'll talk to you later and tell you what I'm doing. You should know that Mary's going to be okay."

"The baby?"

He pauses. "Rapid heart rate, so they're going to monitor Mary at the hospital for a couple of days. Then she can come back."

It's better than I expected, but it's still not good. Delpopolo calls for a guard to come get me. Normally I would argue and try to find out his plan. But I am too depressed to even care. I'm going to go to my room and sleep until the guards wake me for dinner, which I probably will not eat.

I don't know how long I've been out, because it's that heavy stuporous kind of sleep where your mind completely turns off. No dreams. No nothing. I wake slowly to Cyrus banging on my door. "Wake up, Shavonne," he says. "I got something to tell you and you better listen up."

And for some strange reason, even though I'm depressed beyond caring, depressed beyond listening, I swing the door open. I sit on the edge of my bed and listen.

"Back in that van with Cinda, you did good. You did real good. I needed some help and you came through big time."

I don't know what to say, so I stay silent. He stands in the doorway, shifting nervously back and forth in his big scuffed work boots. He looks uneasy having this conversation, but he also looks determined, like he's not leaving until he says what's on his mind.

"So if you ever need help, I'll make sure and be there for you."

I try to get the energy to thank him, but no words come out.

Just before leaving he turns and says, "Oh, in case you're wondering, them goslings made it. They followed their parents downstream to a bigger pond where it's safer. The feathers are just fluff from the nest. Probably raccoons nosing around in it hoping for an egg or two."

53

Connie, my daughter's foster mother, calls me today. I'm so low I don't even have the energy to give her a hard time.

"Hi, Shavonne. How are you doing?"

"Not too good, Connie. How's Jasmine? Can I talk to her?"

"Jasmine's fine. You can talk to her, but I thought we could talk first. Is that okay?"

"Sure." I don't say anything else. If she's got something on her agenda then she's going to have to come out with it.

"Shavonne, I know you think I'm trying to take your daughter away from you." Long pause so that I can say this isn't so. I let the pause hang till she gets the point.

"Well, that's not my plan, Shavonne. I just want

to make sure she's safe and happy. Don't you want that too?"

I hang up in anger and then remember I was supposed to talk to Jasmine. This will be another mark against me as a mother, hanging up on my weekly phone call. Fuck it. I give up.

54

Mr. Delpopolo sits behind his desk, smiling. In front of him is a package about the size of a book, wrapped in shiny red paper. "For you," he says.

"I don't understand."

"Okay, I'll just give it to Kiki instead. She can trade it for five boxes of hair grease."

He's still a wiseass, but I'm not in a joking mood. I work at the paper slowly, trying not to tear it because it's so pretty. It's been a long time since I got a present. Last year the Lion's Club donated some gifts, but they weren't wrapped. It was shampoo and soap and stuff like that. Nothing personal, like I hope this present will be.

It's actually three presents. The first is a beautiful hand-made journal. It's got a real leather cover, kind of plain but very classy. I run my fingers over the stitched design of a stick figure wearing a dress. It's really cool and I love it. It's so cool, I wouldn't even know where to buy something like this. Also there's a real fountain pen with extra ink cartridges. It's just like Delpopolo's. But the third present makes no sense to me. It's a plain nine-by-twelve mailing envelope filled with papers. On the front it says my name.

"What's this?"

"What's it look like?"

"It looks like an envelope filled with paper. What's going on, Mr. D?" The blood in my temples pounds and my heart fills with fear. I know instantly what is in the envelope. How could he do this to me? Why?

"Shavonne, we're almost out of time. Not just for today, but for good. We've got to finish. Do you understand?"

"Yes." I'm looking down now in total fear. I know he's right, but I'm so scared. I undo the clasp on the envelope and slide out a couple of the reports. They're stamped CONFIDENTIAL: PSYCHIATRIC REPORT in red ink. I pick them up with shaky hands.

"What am I supposed to do with these, Mr. D?"

"Whatever you want. It's your history. You can read it, hang on to it, or put it through the shredder. This is the only copy, and the original will be sealed on your birthday, which is in one week, right?"

"Do you do this with all your patients? Like a going-away present?" I don't know what to do or say. Maybe if I keep talking it will become clear.

"No. It's actually against policy for me to give you these papers. But I think you need to see them, or at least hold them."

"Why?" I don't really want to know why, but the question comes out anyway. "Why do I need to see them?"

"Because there's one last thing. Something you've avoided for a long time. It's actually in the reports, and maybe seeing it there will make it easier to talk about."

Then there is silence. I push the beautiful journal and the fountain pen away from me. I will just get up and leave, walk out of the office and never come back. But my legs won't work. They are not my legs. They are made of stone. I remain in the chair.

I remember the "one last thing." It's from my first assignment, the one where I had to write the list of things I felt guilty about. I wrote down mostly typical delinquent-girl stuff: fighting, lying, stealing, skipping school, getting high, having sex, etc. Most of the girls in the Center could have written the same list. Except there was a blank spot on the list. I hadn't been able to write the word because my brain wouldn't even allow me to form the letters. But they're forming now as I speak mechanically, like I am playing some prerecorded message:

"I know what you want from me. I know what you want me to tell you about. It's that thing that I kept off the list and never told anyone about. My secret. You want to hear it? You really want to hear it? Because so help me God, I'll tell you."

"I want to hear it. It's what we have to do today."

The sound of my voice is different. It's like I'm in someone else's body watching myself talk. My words are short, clipped. I must be going crazy. So this is what going crazy is like.

"It's winter, a long time ago. I'm real young, but I don't know how young. Maybe six. I can't explain why I'm not in school. Maybe I don't go to school. I don't know."

Delpopolo doesn't say anything. He just sits there with his hands in his lap. Every now and then he shifts in his chair and the rickety thing squeaks like hell. And the whole time, he stares right at me like he's saying "Go on with the story . . . I want to hear it." But nobody wants to hear this story.

"All I remember is it's cold. So cold the baby is screaming and I can see my breath inside the apartment. The furnace is broken but the electricity works, so Mommy sets up a hot plate in the middle of the living room floor with a big pot of water. She says it will warm us up. She asks me to hold my baby brother, who is wrapped up in blankets. Then she goes out to do a trick and buy drugs. She's been straight for a few days and it's killing her. She practically throws the baby at me and runs out of the apartment. With no jacket on, just a T-shirt and skirt. It's the last time I ever see her."

Delpopolo doesn't even nod or say "Uh-huh" or "Go on" like he usually does. He doesn't interrupt.

"I do my best to sing a lullaby—'Hush little baby, don't say a word, Momma's gonna buy you a mockingbird.' Only I change the words around to say 'Hush, little baby, don't you worry, momma's gonna be back in a hurry.' I know she's not coming back, though. I sing mostly for myself because I'm cold and hungry and scared. I know the baby will wake up soon wanting something to eat and there's nothing in the house. No food or milk."

Delpopolo takes off his tinted glasses and I see his eyes. They're not mean or kind or anything. He's looking at me without any judgment, which is good because I think I'd die if he got even the slightest bit upset or worried. I realize that I've become supersensitive to other people's emotions. I'm always looking to see how they feel about me, like I can only see myself through others' eyes.

I notice that my heart is racing and my legs are shaking back and forth in the chair. I stop talking and feel so scared, like I've already said too much and damned myself forever. I won't finish the story. I say to Delpopolo in a real low voice, "Please . . . Mr D, I don't know what kind of life you've had, but . . ."

And then he gets mad. For the first time, the big shrink shows his real self and says, "That's right. You don't know what kind of life I've had. I agree with you on that."

In a flash I am filled with rage.

"Oh yeah? What kind of troubles have you had, Mr. D? Bad marriage? Child-support payments? Stuck in this hellhole with the rest of us? Well, at least you get to leave at night. At least you have choices. You can find a new wife and have a new family. You can walk out of here any day of the week."

His nostrils flare and an ugly vein pulses in his forehead. He jumps out of his chair, pointing his finger at me.

"You don't know who I am, Shavonne. Just because you overheard something or made some good guesses doesn't mean that you know me. Because a person isn't just the sum of their fuck-ups and their shame. I'm more than that, and so are you. That's what I've been trying to teach you all these months. Now tell me the damn story."

55

I just want him to leave me alone, to let me off the hook. It makes me want to curl up in a ball and die. Why is this fat prick pushing me around? The anger rises again and blankets the fear for another brief moment. I call up even more anger.

"Fuck you, Delpopolo," I say. "I'm through." I stand up to leave, ready to blow right out of there. But then Delpopolo changes his tone. He doesn't yell, but his voice gets stronger, like he's ready for an argument.

He says, "Fuck you too. You act so damn tough, but you can't even do this one thing. If you're so damn tough, then sit down and finish the story."

I scream, "Yeah, well, you don't know what kind of life *I've* had! You have no fucking idea, Mr. D. If you did, you wouldn't be asking me to go on!"

His voice is calm now. Kind, almost. "It's now or never, Shavonne. You *can* do this. I wouldn't have asked if I didn't believe you could. If you quit now," he says, "you're on your own."

It's a threat that goes right through me like a bullet made of ice. It chills me with fear. I know what he says is true: this is my last chance. I need to tell this one last secret or it will probably destroy me. I try to bring back the hate and put it all on him, even though I know he hasn't ever done anything to me. It's confusing, and the stress is so intense that I feel like my nose will bleed. It's not logical, but I see now that it's him who raped me when I was eleven. It's him who took me away from school in a cop car to a foster home where I was molested again. It's him who burned my arms with matches for crying too much. It's him who threw me on the hard floor and busted my teeth. It's him I hate, and I tell him so. "I hate you," I scream. "You motherfucker, I hate you! Do you hear me, Delpopolo? I hate you!"

He sits back and says, "Continue, please." Just like that. Like this was his plan: to get me angry and screaming. It's crazy, but I do as he says. I sit back in my chair. I don't curse at him anymore or try to escape. Instead, I finish the story.

"I dropped the baby," I say flatly. The words coming out slow and heavy, like each syllable is a sack of cement dropping off a building. *Thump.* "I was supposed to watch him, but he started crying and squirming out of my arms and I accidentally dropped him. He fell and knocked over the pot so all that boiling water dumped on him. I didn't mean to drop him, but that doesn't matter. All that matters is, because of me, my baby brother got his skin scalded off his legs. He went to the hospital and I got sent to foster care. I stopped talking to other people. I heard voices. They sent me to a psychiatric hospital for a long time."

I finish speaking, maybe forever. Because this time, I am broken. Completely. Saying the words, telling the story, it doesn't heal me like I hoped. Instead, it shatters me, and my whole body shakes. There are no tears. Just violent shaking, like I am freezing to death. I am so cold, and I can't stop shaking.

A low sickening moan escapes me. It rises in pitch slowly, changing to some kind of primitive scream. Finally, it explodes out of me in a raw shriek that heaves and wracks my body like I'm having convulsions. Something awful and ugly and diseased is trying to leave my body and it wants to kill me on the way out. It's like labor, only the end is death instead of birth. My face runs with mucus and hot tears. I am so broken, all I can do is take the convulsions and hope that it will all end.

Please, God, make this end. I can't take it anymore.

56

A hand reaching out to me. I can't see it well because my eyes are blurry from crying. It's got to be Delpopolo's; the part of me that is still able to think figures that I am in his office, and he's the only other person present. The hand reaches across the expanse of the desk and gently takes my hand. It happens so slowly. In slow motion. Even though it's just a couple feet of desktop, it takes such a long time, so long for someone to reach me.

Delpopolo's large soft hand closes around my own, which feels small and childlike. A flicker of memory: I am six years old, playing a game with Marcus. I hide his tiny hand in mine and say, "Where's your hand, baby? Where did your hand go?" Peals of laughter from Marcus as I uncover and show him his tiny beautiful little fingers, which he wiggles to show that they have been returned to him. The power of a hand held inside another, like nesting dolls or stacked shells.

I realize that, aside from violent takedowns and having my hair braided by Cinda, no one has touched me since I've been locked up. How strange to go through life without touch. In its own way it is like going without water for years. Impossible, I know, but there it is.

Delpopolo has taken off his tinted glasses and I can see he is crying. Is he crying for his own miserable life or for mine? Doesn't matter. Like a drowning person, I grab for him, because at the moment, he is all that stands between me and madness or self-destruction. There is still the desk between us, so I grab what is available: his fat hand. I bury my face in it and cry like I've never cried before. Tears pour out of my eyes and run into his outstretched hand. Like he can absorb the pain and the grief by catching my tears. Or maybe just share it for a moment and then let it go. I don't care, just so long as there is that touch.

We stay like that for a long time. He brings out his other hand and I take that one too, clasping both of his wrists and burrowing my face into his palms. He says over and over, "It's all right, Shavonne. It wasn't your fault. You're going to be okay. You're going to be just fine."

I grab his wrists tighter and bury my face deeper into his palms. I gasp for air between sobs and say, "I'm sorry, I'm so sorry." I don't know if I'm apologizing to Marcus for what I did, or to Mr. D. And still, Delpopolo keeps saying those words: "It's all right, Shavonne. It wasn't your fault. You're going to be okay. You're going to be just fine. It wasn't your fault."

57

Nothing. I have no real thoughts or feel-ings. I pass the days by staring out the window or pretending to read a book. Choi got fined five hundred dollars and was given a five-day suspension for fucking up my face and hurting Mary. Tyreena, Kiki, and the other girls are celebrating, singing that shit from *The Wizard of Oz* about the wicked witch being dead, but I don't care. I see now that Choi has nothing to do with my problems. She isn't anybody to me; she's just a distraction, like so many other things I've wasted my time on.

My eighteenth birthday is three days away, but I refuse to talk to my law guardian or Susan, the DSS worker. I won't talk to Connie or Jasmine, either. I can't deal with problems that are too big. The only thing in my head close to a plan is not to have a plan. I will go into court and say nothing. I will nod to the judge. I will let the whole thing play out without help from me. The judge will give me a new assault charge, for Ms. Williams, or not. He will send me to adult prison, or not. I will be released on my eighteenth birthday, or not. None of it matters, really.

58

Ms. Choi is back from her suspension. She says she's got something planned for me on account of how I cost her five hundred cash plus a week of pay.

"Eye for an eye, little girl. You messed up my life, now I'm gonna mess up yours. And in the end, it's your word against mine. You think anyone's gonna believe your lyin' ass?"

One look at the other guards tells me they're in on it. Or they'll cover for her. Same difference. She calls our movement on the radio and leads me to the cafeteria for work duty. Only, the cafeteria is dark; no one is there.

She turns on the lights and points to a prep table with a bunch of vegetables: heads of lettuce, greenish tomatoes, and a cucumber. She unlocks the knife drawer and gets a small paring knife, puts it on the table with the veggies. The thin blade of the knife gleams under the fluorescent lighting.

This is bad. I see now that she's crazier than I thought. She planned this. She is watching me, grinning, rubbing her hands together. She set the whole thing up and this is part of her pleasure.

"Go cut up them vegetables, Shavonne. We ain't got all day."

It's like she's reading from a script. Her tone is casual, friendly even. I don't understand what's happening because my brain isn't working quickly enough. But I know enough not to touch the knife.

"I can't. I'm on restriction. I lost my work privileges."

"I don't care about no restriction. You do what I tell you, girl."

"But Ms. Choi, I can get a level three." I look around for help, but there's no one. Just me and Choi.

"Girl, I don't give a shit about no level three."

"What's this about, then? Not vegetables." I try to find some way out of this, but I'm trapped. Either I pick up the knife and get set up for a weapons charge, or I get another concussion or a broken arm for not following directions.

"That's right, smart girl. It ain't about vegetables. Now pick up the damn knife and start choppin'!" She screams at me, desperate, coming unhinged. Then she calms herself, grinning madly, and turns up a bloody palm for inspection.

"Doesn't matter, 'cause you already cut me. See?" I see. I am fucked. She will push the emergency button on her radio and wait for the guards. Then she'll rush at me, grabbing the knife on the way if I haven't already grabbed it. It will be a good story. A believable story, with witnesses.

Choi takes her radio out of its holster and shows me the little orange button called the pin. But before she can push it, the doors swing open with a whoosh of air. In walks Cyrus with a tool belt and a power drill.

Ms. Choi is beyond pissed. She stares him down and says, "Get back to the unit, *Cyrus*. They need you to help with bathroom breaks. We're fine here."

Cyrus acts like he doesn't even hear. "What, Ms. Choi? I didn't hear you. I gotta do some work here, but I won't make no noise. It's all wrenches and screwdrivers. You won't know I'm here." He kneels down by one of the freezers and removes a panel, starts tinkering. I step away from the table and the knife.

Ms. Choi is furious. "Shavonne, get back at that table! And you, Cyrus, who told you to come down here? There ain't no problem with that thing!"

"Oh, these old freezers are temperamental, Ms. Choi. Every now and then they need the dust blowed away and the compressor adjusted. It cost this place a hundred bucks just to get an HVAC guy to come out and take a look. But I said I'd do it from now on. I kind of like to play around with 'em, if you can believe it." He winks. I wink back and smile broadly. I decide that Cyrus is my hero.

Choi glares at him. No doubt she's trying to melt his face with her pure meanness. As she pushes open the cafeteria doors, the self-inflicted cut on her hand leaves an angry smear of blood. At the bottom of the smear a single scarlet rivulet collects and travels down a few inches before stopping. I am relieved to have escaped such a close call with Ms. Choi, but I fear that the blood on the door is a sign, a warning. *If you stay here, you will bleed.* Maybe it will not scrub off easily and will stand through time to show the truth of this place, but I doubt it.

59

A knock on my door. It's Ms. Williams. Her face is pretty again. I am glad about this because she is a good person. She never treated us badly. She tried to do right, even if no one wanted her to. I'd like to apologize to her, but I'm just too tired. I can hardly keep myself sitting upright.

She walks in, followed by Mr. Delpopolo. He says, "Hello, Shavonne."

I wave but don't feel like talking. I already heard that I'll be leaving on my eighteenth birthday, but I don't know how to feel about this. On the one hand it's what I wanted: to go home. The only problem is, I've got no home to go to.

"I've got something important for you." He has a thick envelope in his shirt pocket, which he pats with his hand. "You remember the other week I said I had to make some phone calls?"

I draw my knees up to my chest and nod. I wrap my arms around my knees and look at the far wall. I don't think I want any more surprises. I want to be left alone. So I can think.

"Well, those calls were about this letter. It's from your brother. He wants to see you."

My ears hiss like the air has been sucked out of the room. Before I can say anything, Delpopolo tosses the envelope onto my bed. He and Ms. Williams sit there looking at me, watching to see what I might do—scream, fight, go crazy? No. There is nothing left in me. I feel the weight of the letter pressing down on my mattress, though I know this is impossible. A letter from my brother. But it can't be. I say the words in my head: *My brother.* Maybe my lips move.

I say, "I don't have a brother. I *had* a brother. I hurt him and he got taken away. We don't get to be family anymore. Weren't you listening when I told you the story?"

Mr. D and Ms. Williams look at each other with concern.

"You're still family. Your brother lives in a foster home in the city. Like I said, he wants to see you. He wants to get to know you, Shavonne."

Mr. D and Ms. Williams sit there for what feels like a long time, probably because I look so freaked out. Thank God they don't try and talk to me. After a while they nod to each other and walk out. It's strange, these two working together. They're very different, but I like them both.

Mr. D has a guard keep a real close eye on me for the

rest of the day. I think he's worried I might try and kill myself. I stay awake the whole night looking at that envelope. I hold it next to my heart, trying to feel some of what could be inside. I don't dare open it, though. Too scared. Is it a letter to finish me off and damn me to hell? Or is it really what Mr. D says? How can my brother possibly care about me after what I did to him? I trace the name and return address with my fingers as though I am reading Braille. *Marcus Washington. 312 Porter Avenue, Apt. 3B.* But my fingers never get any farther. Each time they trace back to the beginning, to his name. Marcus. Marcus Washington. My brother, Marcus.

60

Time passes quickly now. I still haven't read the letter, but I carry it around with me. It's taped to the inside of my journal next to a picture of my daughter.

It's getting harder to think of Jasmine as my daughter, because the distance between us is increasing every day. We have no real history together other than a couple of days in the hospital. Every week I spend in lockup is another one she spends with her foster mother. I imagine the two of them reading books, watching Disney movies, snuggling under a blanket. It makes me sad to think of what I'm missing. I'm also jealous, because Jasmine is experiencing something I always dreamed of. I am ashamed of this feeling. I know it's selfish, but I can't deny it. Imagine being jealous of your own daughter's safety and happiness!

61

I call on the phone.

"Connie, it's me, Shavonne." My voice is shaking badly, but I will go on. I will go through with it. Because I have to. For Jasmine.

"Are you all right, Shavonne? Did something happen?"

I can hear the worry in Connie's voice. She's used to me being hostile or defensive.

"Listen, Connie. Don't interrupt, because this is going to be hard for me to say. You love Jasmine, right? I mean, you really love her. Like she's your own, right?"

"Why, of course I do, Shavonne. Are you in some kind of trouble? You're not planning to do something, Shavonne, are you? Maybe I should talk to that doctor you've been seeing."

"No. Shut up and listen, Connie. I need you to hear me and I can only say this once. I want you to be Jasmine's mother for good because I just can't do it. It's not fair for her to have me as a mother because I'm too messed up. I want her to be safe and happy. You'll give that to her, won't you?"

Silence. Then Jasmine starts talking in the background, asking Connie for some juice. Only she doesn't call her Connie. She calls her mommy. Connie doesn't answer until Jasmine chatters, "Mommy, Mommy, Mommy, juice, juice, juice!" Then Connie says softly, "Okay, baby, here's your juice."

That's all I need to hear, because it tells me I'm right to walk away. Connie really has become Jasmine's mother. All I'm doing is acknowledging it. I didn't think my heart could break any more, but apparently it can. Instead of answering my question, Connie starts crying. She wails into that phone just like her own heart has been broken, and I can tell she's crying for me. She should be crying out of happiness, because I know she wants to adopt Jasmine more than anything in the world. But she's crying for me because I am giving up my baby.

"Oh, Shavonne, I'll keep her safe and I'll make sure she has a happy life, but I'm so sorry. I know that I should be happy and I suppose I am, but I'm also sorry. I'm so sorry, Shavonne."

"I'm sorry too, Connie. I'm sorry for lots of things. Goodbye."

62

I go to court and sign the papers for Jasmine to be adopted. Delpopolo stops meeting with me because I have nothing to say. I don't argue or curse. I answer questions either yes, no, or I don't know. And I don't play games or avoid anything. There's simply nothing to say, and I think he knows this. So instead of meeting with me, he checks in with the guards every day.

"Has she been eating?"

"Yes, a little bit from each meal."

"How about sleep?"

"Some. She stays up late writing in her journal, but then sleeps through wake-up and chores. We let it go because she's out of here in a couple of days anyway. There's not much we can hold over her head to motivate her."

63

There's a lot I don't know about or understand. Like saying goodbye. The first person to come by my bedroom is Ms. Stokes. I'm still sullen and shut-down, afraid of what lies ahead of me. This is new for me, because I've always been afraid of the past. I never even bothered thinking about the future.

Ms. Stokes pretends everything is normal. She says, "Happy birthday, Shavonne. You can go ahead and be depressed or rude or any way you like. But I've got my girl stuff here and I'm not leaving until I do your hair and your nails. So move over."

She opens up her kit and gives me a total pedicure, or what I think a total pedicure is, never having had one before. I'm embarrassed by the attention until she says, "Look, Shavonne. This is a small thing. Just one small thing I can do for you out of respect. Because you tried to protect that poor pregnant girl when things got out of hand. And you protected Cinda, too, when no one else ever did."

As she braids my hair she tells me I'm going to grow up to be a strong woman. She says that my life is a book with only a few finished chapters. And even though they have been bad, I can work hard to write the next ones and make them better. It sounds nice, and I appreciate her spending this time with me and telling me something hopeful, even though I don't really believe it.

But before she says goodbye and leaves my life forever, Ms. Stokes hands me a small color photo of a light-skinned newborn baby with wisps of curly brown hair and impossibly chubby cheeks. "Your grandson?" I ask.

"No. Guess again." She's smiling, like she knows I'll figure out the answer and it will please me. And as I do figure it out, I smile too. A big broad happy smile, the first in a long time.

"For real? Mary's baby? Ramón? He's healthy?"

"Yes." Just one word, but she says it so proud. Like it's proof of something. What can it prove? That there is still reason to hope? That good things are possible? For Mary? For me? Before I can think about it, Ms. Stokes gives me a quick hug and says goodbye. "Take care of yourself, Shavonne. Be a strong woman." She leaves me standing in my small bedroom, clutching the picture and feeling so many things: happiness, sadness, fear, regret, and yes, the beginnings of something like hope.

64

I'm now on a Greyhound bus headed to a shelter/independent living program in the city. The bus is packed. I scan the aisles and find one empty seat. It's next to a large black woman, who motions for me to take it. I walk down the aisle and feel everyone's eyes on me. I'm wearing new clothes Ms. Williams purchased for me at Old Navy.

They're nice clothes, and I feel special today only because of them. The down jacket is white with pink faux fur around the hood. And the jeans must look good on me, because some boys turn their heads as I walk past them. But mostly I feel nothing as the bus cruises away. And that's okay, because I think I can deal with nothing.

The big woman next to me changes seats so I can look out the window. I try to object, but she puts up a big fleshy arm and says, "Girl, I seen almost everything there is to see out them windows. Now you sit there and look while

I take myself a nap." I like her voice because it reminds me of someone, but I can't remember who. Everything seems so distant.

Trees line the roads in different stages of readiness for spring. I see the buds starting to break open with the faintest hint of green. I try to relate to this slow awakening, but I can't. It's like looking at a beautiful wilderness scene in a book and saying, "Oh, that's nice."

I wish I knew the trees by their names. Back at the Center Cyrus taught us about the trees on campus. He used to point and call out, "Hemlock, ladies, and over there, maple, pin oak. Those two are walnut. And there, shagbark hickory. You see that one? That's American ironwood. Also called hornbeam and musclewood, because the bark looks like it's got muscles."

I don't know why I'm thinking about Cyrus. Maybe because of the trees. Or maybe because he helped me in the cafeteria when no one else could. But I think it's because he too seemed out of place and trapped. Maybe he will quit and go work on a farm somewhere. It could be a farm with a horse to plow the fields the old-fashioned way. And one day he'll be out there in the fields when the sun sets and lights everything on fire with orange and gold, and his shadow will stretch out forever. That's a nice thought and I'm trying to hang on to it, but it's already fading.

The Greyhound is passing houses now. Nice houses, big fancy things, but I don't know their names. Could be Victorian or something else. It occurs to me that I don't know much about the world outside of the Center and my old neighborhood. How will I manage? How will I find my way?

In my lap, fingers are working to break open the seal of an envelope. The fingers are beautiful, slender, and smooth, with nut-brown skin. The nails, gently curved and lacquered, are not long but appear well cared for. Are they mine? They can't be the old woman's, because her skin is a very dark black. Plus her fingers are short and chubby. They must be my fingers. But I can't really feel them. I don't know what's happening. I am drifting into some other place like a daydream, but I'm also reading the pages, which are spread on my lap. And now there's a picture, one of those small rectangular school pictures.

A voice penetrates the trance. "That your boyfriend?" It's the woman sitting next to me. She has awakened from her nap and is trying to start a conversation.

"What? Excuse me?"

"I said, is that your boyfriend? He sure is handsome."

"Um, no. It's not my boyfriend."

"Well, then who is it? If you don't mind me asking."

"I don't mind. It's my brother."

"What's your brother's name?"

I think the name in my head but I can't say it. *Marcus. My brother's name is Marcus.* The woman is looking at me with concern because tears are coming, streaming down my cheeks in hot rivers. Tears that are equal parts salt and fear, water and sorrow. I see now what tears are made of, at least my own. And I understand why I haven't been able to get better. Because I am made of equal parts fear and sorrow.

And this makes me cry even harder, for all of it. All of it. Mary and her pregnant belly. Cinda and her burned-down house. Samantha's birthday cake. Cyrus and those fucking geese. All those people whose lives I passed through: Ms. Williams. Mr. Delpopolo. Jasmine. Mona, who held my hands and talked softly to me that day at the hospital. I have passed through all their lives and they are gone. Have I gone too?

The woman next to me touches my upper arm. "Lord have mercy! What have we here?" She's looking at me with sympathy. She sets down her purse and pulls me to her. She's soft but strong and I am not able to resist. I am grateful that I am, at long last, not able to resist.

"Let it all loose, girl! Whatever it is, let it *loose.* Let it come on out and we'll take a look and see what it is!" She looks up at the other passengers, who are staring at us, and shouts, "Ain't you never seen nobody feelin' sad? Shoot. Nosy sonsabitches!"

Eventually she sets me back against my own seat and pulls some tissues out of her purse. She talks softly to me for the rest of the trip, telling me that it's always been a hard world for a woman, no matter if she's young and pretty or fat and old. She tells me that it's going to be okay.

"How do you know?" I ask. I hear the desperation in my voice, as though the rest of my life hinges on the answer to this one question. It's a child's question, really. How do you know that everything's going to be okay? How do you know that the world isn't going to crush me?

"Because, child, I know at least one person loves you." She pulls out the small rectangular picture from between our two seats and returns it to me. Could it be true?

I cry again, but this time it's out of hope. I am hoping that this big kind woman knows what she's talking about, and I think she does. I think I can trust her. And I think I already do trust Ms. Williams, and Connie, and Cyrus, and Mona, and Mr. Delpopolo. It's a good list.

65

The bus pulls into the station with a whoosh of air from the brakes and suspension. I am afraid to get out but all the passengers are gone. The driver is waiting patiently for me, probably because he's afraid I'll start crying again.

Down the steps and into the rain. There are people everywhere. Some are shaking hands or giving hugs. But none of these people mean anything to me. I am alone.

Then, through all the anonymous faces, there is one that I know. Well, I don't know it, but I recognize it. It is familiar. A boy, thirteen years old, wearing a backpack and a rain jacket. Waving. Walking over to me. Smiling but frightened. Frightened that maybe I will not recognize him. Frightened that I will not accept him. Or is that what I'm feeling?

"Shavonne?"

"Marcus?"

We stand there smiling at each other. Then Marcus throws his arms around me awkwardly. He squeezes me half to death and I try to hug him back but I can't get my arms around his backpack. I can tell he is crying and doesn't want me to see. I try to look at his face, but he is still hugging me tightly and won't let go. I am crying, too, and the tears are mixing with raindrops. They taste lightly salted.

"I missed you, Shavonne. I've missed you so much."

"Me too, Marcus. Me too."

"But everything is all messed up because . . ."

Marcus starts to tell me why things are messed up, but I cut him off. "It's okay, Marcus. I've got a plan." I put my arm around his narrow shoulders and we start walking away. I don't even know where we're going. Marcus leans into me like he trusts my weight to hold him up. Like he trusts me. It feels strange and powerful and scary, all at the same time.

"We're going to be okay," I tell Marcus. I say it again and again to reassure him. I say it just to hear the words. And it's like someone else is saying it, telling *me*. "We're going to be okay," I say once again. It sounds good because, for the first time, the words are believable, like they might be true. Could they be true? I think so. For a moment I think they might be magic words, like they hold some special healing power if only I can say them enough times. I want to tell Marcus about this, but I am afraid it will sound silly and become untrue. Which is crazy, really, because it's not about the words at all. It's about forgiveness. Or maybe it's about faith. Or maybe I don't even know, which is okay too. Because all that matters is that I am with my brother, and we are walking together toward something new.

about the author

Shawn Goodman based *Something Like Hope* on his experiences working as a psychologist in a girls' juvenile justice facility. He lives in upstate New York with his wife and daughters.